THE
WOMAN
IN THE
GAZEBO

Joy de Livre

The Woman in the Gazebo
Joy de Livre

Copyright © 2020 Joy de Livre

First Edition

Library of Congress Cataloging-in-Publication Data
Softcover ISBN: 978-1-4218-3682-9

Published by 1st World Publishing
P.O. Box 2211, Fairfield, Iowa 52556
tel: 641-209-5000 • fax: 866-440-5234
web: www.1stworldpublishing.com

ONE

The red Honda CRV emerged from behind the bend, pulled to the curb and stopped. I jumped into the front passenger seat and wrapped my arms around Martin's neck, resting my head against his shoulder.

"Why did you slam the door, Marie?" he tapped my elbow lying on his chest. "How many times do I need to say it? Jesus, I feel mad like hell!"

"I'm so sorry, I rushed because of the traffic."

"It is not about the door, Marie! But you should always close the door softly," he sighed. "I'm worried about you. I want you to be strong and independent, in case something happens to me, since ..." Fire trucks drove by with their sirens on. I could feel his words vibrating inside his chest, but I couldn't discern them.

"... I am ready to end my career, and end my life," I heard him say as the noise subsided, and then for a while I heard silence. "I cannot live like this," he said. "They are not observing OSHA requirements, and their technology is ancient. It's like the Middle Ages."

"Can something be done about it?"

"Yes! Get the hell out of there," he said.

I looked at him, my arm still wrapped around his neck, "Well, there has to be a better job for you, Martin," I said.

"Well Marie, when you go out there and apply for jobs, then you can advise me," he mocked. "Do you know how many applications I submitted and how few interviews I was invited to?"

"I know," I said fast, afraid he might list them.

Martin parked the car. He put his arm around my shoulders as we walked to our apartment. He washed his hands, sat on the couch and turned on the television. I went to the kitchen.

"Dinner is ready," I put a jar with daisies on the table and lit the candles.

"I want to sit in front of the television and eat!" Martin said without diverting his eyes from the TV screen.

I scooped some potatoes, tofu sticks, and salad and placed the plate on a tray.

"Here you are," I put the tray on Martin's lap, and sat at the dining table to eat.

Through the flickering candlelight, I watched Martin in front of me, sitting, eating, and switching channels. The way he watched with full focus, his swimmer's shoulders back, his back straight.

I remembered standing by the window, watching him park his car by the curb and walk towards the building entrance. He walked a smooth kind of walk, which didn't disturb the air.

"I came to tell you that I cannot go with you to the play tonight," in my memory I clearly heard him say.

"But I got us great tickets," I said.

"Go with someone else," he said and paused.

"Why?" I gasped for air.

"I have a guest, a visitor from Chicago, my father's friend's daughter. Come," He walked me towards the window and pointed, "She is in my car, waiting," he smiled. "I've got to go."

"No!" I gasped. "I cannot go to the theater. You and your guest go," I grabbed the tickets from my purse, "Take them, please."

"No, no, no!" He pushed my hand away. "You go. It is Cat on a Hot Tin Roof."

"I cannot go! Take the tickets please," I begged.

"It's your favorite play, I will not go without you."

"I will not go without you," I said, and thought for a second. "Why don't you and your lady guest take these tickets, and I will get another one for myself?"

He stared at the floor. "Okay. You bring the tickets tonight."

I walked him downstairs and to the front of the building and watched him walk five yards along the path towards his car. "Martin," I yelled behind him. He stopped walking, turned around and looked at me. I listened to the breeze rustling through the soft holly bushes framing the path and a bunch of sparrows chirping, startled as he passed by. I had called his name with a clear intention to say something urgent but couldn't spell out a word. Instead, I stood in no man's land with a feeling in my heart but no thought in my head.

In my body there was a paralyzing pain, and there was a faint hope fading minute-by-minute as the time to meet them at the theater neared. I hung on to a thinning thread of hope which I saw in the fact that he didn't want to go without me. By the time he approached me with a curvaceous blond resembling a young Brigitte Bardot holding onto his arm, I was numbed to *the point of extinction. Miraculously, my love, though bodiless and ethereal, still pulsated life.*

That night as he sat next to Brigitte Bardot in orchestra seats, from the back of the theater I saw only him, his shoulders broad, his back straight. Except when he leaned towards her to whisper something into her ear, when his face submerged again and again into the abundance of her blond waves.

As that memory faded away, I felt the softness of Martin's soul shine right there in front of me on the couch and was thankful. I left my dinner on the table unfinished and walked to the couch, knelt on the floor, and embraced Martin from behind, my head on his shoulder.

"Don't you worry, we will figure out something," I said.

"Easy for you to say. You close your eyes and meditate, you do not live in this world," he said, still looking at the TV screen.

"What do you see ideally happening?"

"Having my own business!"

"That is a great idea," I said.

"I can utilize the best technology, I can use the best materials, I can uphold the highest standards in my profession according to my training, make people happy and enjoy what I do. I take seriously my profession. It is important, and it can be effective. It can be lucrative too. It should be lucrative. I didn't expect that after investing hundreds of thousands on my education I would not be able to live the kind of life my colleagues do. I've got good hands. It is beautiful work really, work that to some might seem too scientific, but I chose it because of its artistic side. For me, it is a form of art."

I noticed that he forgot to switch the channels when the

commercials started, and although his eyes were directed towards the screen, it seemed like he was not watching TV.

"At least three rooms, an intra-oral camera, digital radiology, completely computerized," he looked towards the balcony door at drooping pine tree branches swaying in the wind.

"Let's do it," I said.

"How?" He looked at me.

"The same way other people do."

"Other people have money," he said.

"Not all of them," I said. "Let's see what it takes."

"Marie, I know you do not like money, but that is what it takes. Money! And we do not have wealthy parents to help us. Do you know that half of my classmates had parents who paid for their education, and who after graduation inherited their parents' businesses? I don't have anyone to help me."

"I can help," I said softly.

"By sitting with your eyes closed, meditating?" he mocked.

"I can find a job," I said.

"Find a job? $10 per hour? You do not have good earning potential. You have two masters' degrees, yet you cannot help me." He shook his head in disbelief.

"There's got to be a solution," I said.

"Yes, there is a solution."

"What?" I felt my eyes growing bigger.

"Lottery," he said.

"Good idea!" I clapped my hands. "Let's get tickets."

"I got one at Come and Go," he said quietly.

"People win the lottery all the time." I stroked his arm.

"That hope is keeping me alive," he said.

"Maybe this time you will win," I smiled.

"Maybe. But if I don't, I will leave everything behind. I will quit this job and kill myself," Martin looked at the TV screen without blinking.

"Let's go to bed. Tomorrow things will look much brighter," I said.

"I am not going to bed until the last late show host tells me 'good night,'" he said.

"Good night," I kissed Martin on the cheek and went to the bedroom. I lay down in the darkness listening to the late night talk shows with intermittent advertisements.

In the morning, Martin got up and went to work. I took a thermometer from under my pillow and slid it under my tongue. *Why am I even doing this?* I wondered, and entered 97 Fahrenheit in the ovulation chart, then closed my eyes to meditate.

In the middle of my meditation, I heard heavy footsteps coming up the stairs, and the thud of a rolled newspaper at our door. I finished my meditation with a few minutes of rest, then picked up the *Andover Daily News* from the landing and spread it on the living room floor.

I looked at the ads, "Martin is right, mostly $10 per hour."

I noticed that with my masters in psychology I could get paid $20 per hour, which made me feel hopeful. But then, hidden in fine print, I saw "five years of experience needed." *It doesn't hurt to try*, I thought, and emailed my resume.

TWO

There was not much traffic on this section of South Adams, except in front of the DailyFix coffee shop a block down the street. George stood at the curb in front of his house, looking at the commotion on the congested DailyFix parking lot.

People rushed in and rushed out, their hands full of coffee cups and pastries. He watched a woman place two cups of coffee on the top of her Chevrolet to free her hands to open the car door, and momentarily drive away in a hurry. George flinched and made a motion as if to catch the tumbling cups from the distance, and realizing he couldn't help, lifted his arms in resignation as coffee steam lingered above a shimmering black puddle.

The clock on the courthouse announced nine o'clock and the crowd didn't seem to be dwindling, so he slowly walked towards the coffee shop. The waiting line stretched to the door.

He squeezed inside. Standing against the glass door, he tried hard to think about quiet places, his backyard garden, his gazebo with rambling roses climbing up each column. *I'll have my coffee there*, he decided, as he kept stepping out of the way each time someone walked in or out through the door.

"Cappuccino macchiato," George finally placed his order.

"For here or to go?" the plump girl with rosy cheeks behind the counter asked with a smile.

"For here," George was surprised to hear himself say.

"Please take a seat," she pointed at the tables lined up along the wall.

To avoid people standing in line, George sat on the farthest chair against the wall, facing the crowd.

The girl brought his order quicker than he expected.

"Thank you," George said, distracted by people looking at him.

At first he nodded and mumbled, "Morning, morning..." Then he thought that perhaps he got cream on his mustaches, and he kept wiping them off with a paper napkin.

An older gentleman held his coffee in one hand and pulled his glasses out of his shirt pocket with the other. Standing by the table, facing George, he put his glasses on and leaned forward.

"I might be getting senile before my time, or everyone here is looking at me," George said.

The gentleman silently pointed at the wall behind George and moved his head closer to check out the details.

George turned around.

On the wall, right behind his head, there was a poster of a woman in a red bikini holding a steaming cup of DailyFix coffee.

"Everyone likes me hot," the man pointed as he read the words above the woman's head, his emerald ring reflecting a spectrum of colors across the poster on the wall.

"I came here a few times, never even noticed. It must be a new thing," George said.

"Howard, Howard Blake. I live a few blocks down the street," he unbuttoned his linen jacket and sat across from George.

"George Harris," George nodded.

"Interesting, don't you think, George?" Howard said, motioning with his head towards the poster.

George awkwardly turned around and gave the poster another look. The feminine form showed every curve, every subtle layer of muscles on her arms, legs, and pecs. Nuances of mounds barely hid beneath the delicate fabric of her minimal bikini. *Body-builder*, George suspected with a smirk.

"What do you think?" Howard watched George evaluate the poster.

"Kitsch!" George hissed.

"Kitsch?"

"Not art!" George concluded and sipped his cappuccino.

"It is kitsch," Howard agreed. "But isn't kitsch a form of art?"

"It is, for those who do not know true art."

"All these people looking at the poster are drawn to it. It gives them some sort of pleasure, obviously. Isn't that what art does?"

"That is what commercialism does. Put out the picture of a naked woman, and you cannot squeeze yourself inside through the door to get a cup of coffee."

"You think these people are purchasing coffee inspired by the poster?" asked Howard.

"Yes. Subconsciously. It is a well-known fact."

"That is fantastic!" Howard clapped. "That is the true art."

"True art?" George objected. "You must be kidding!"

"On the contrary, George, I'm talking about the true art of marketing."

"Now that's a stretch!"

"How about yourself, George? Coming here because of the poster? Subconsciously, of course."

"I would rather look at Rembrandt."

"Ha! You like them plump, like Danae?" Howard teased.

"The point is, I like art, not porn," George slurped his cappuccino.

"I see no difference, George. Some would argue that porn is a form of art," Howard said.

"True. Hard to comprehend!" George shook his head.

"Isn't art about expressing ourselves?"

"Expressing ourselves, yes, but in a beautiful way!" George said.

"What's beautiful to you may not be beautiful to me."

"Howard, art is supposed to uplift the mind, heart and soul, and bring human awareness to a higher level of functioning. Pornography brings mind, heart and spirit to the lower levels of animalistic instinct. I wish there were an instrument to measure what these people feel looking at this naked woman."

"Naked?" Howard put his glasses back on and looked at the poster.

"Almost!" George said. "You can see through the fabric."

"I cannot," Howard said.

"Cannot?" George took a long look at the bikini-covered areas on the poster.

"What do you feel?" Howard asked.

"I feel people are choosing low-level art, that's what I feel."

"George, what do you think these people around here are feeling?"

"I don't know, but I suspect the tests would show adrenalin rush."

"You mean like fight-or-flight? That's when people are in danger, isn't it?"

"Look Howard, I'm an expert in art. I'm no expert in the carnal impulses in humans. Those are leftover genes from when people were animals, which I fondly call baboon genes."

A big police officer stormed into the coffee shop. "What's going on here? Clear the entrance!" he roared, trying to squeeze himself in. People quickly pushed aside. "I said, what's going on here?" he demanded.

"Nothing, officer."

"Everything is okay. Why?"

"Why? We've got vehicles outside double parked and triple parked! We've got a fire hazard inside, way above maximum capacity!" the officer's voice boomed through the packed room. "Why are you here?" he confronted a young man. "Explain yourself!"

"Getting my coffee, officer, what's the problem?"

"Just making sure you're not causing trouble, young man" the officer looked around. "What is that, now?" he eyes caught sight of the poster. His eyes bulged. His face paled. He froze. "Pornography to go along with the coffee?" he mumbled.

"No, officer ..." the rosy-cheeked barista said.

"She's pretty," a businessman nodded.

"That bikini girl will excite you and hurt you," the officer's voice trembled. "I'm here to protect you! Alright now, anyone who doesn't have a chair, clear out! Clear the premises at once! Move, I said!" He herded customers out the door. "It's my duty," he reminded them. In minutes, the shop became almost empty, and the officer disappeared outside.

"Baboon genes?" Howard turned to George.

"Survival of the species."

"Sorry to disagree, George. The truth is, beauty is superficial, it is difficult to define, and it is highly overrated. Utterly fleeting. Therefore, we stick with what matters — business, commerce, and affluence. The masses know what they want, and we give it to them. Whatever they want!"

"Shallow like a puddle," George shook his head. "And by the way, Howard, what makes you an expert in this matter?"

"And, my friend, you are no expert either," Howard said to George and looked around. "Good morning, young man," he turned to a customer sitting at the next table. "You looked at the girl on the poster?"

"Why? Is it prohibited? What is it with everybody today? First that officer and now you."

"Just wondering how you feel when you look, that's all." Howard explained nicely.

"Like a free man!" the young man raised his arms up in the air.

"Ha, ha ha," George laughed full heartedly. "So maybe it isn't even that they like what they see. Maybe they just like the freedom to look at it, since it is on the wall. Herd mentality!" George scoffed.

"I would like to believe that people look for practical reasons," Howard said.

"Like the deeply rooted desire to multiply?"

"People multiply no matter what. For me, I like commerce. Porn is commerce, nudity is commerce, the bikini girl on the wall is commerce. Commerce is art."

"On the surface it might look like art is no more nor less than lucrative commerce, and ignorant masses see it that way. It sells. But none of that, Howard, none of that is art. Not even close. Art lasts through the ages. It is pure, and it satisfies higher impulses!"

"George, I accept that as your personal viewpoint, but the masses may think differently. And that's what matters. As a businessman and as a curious person, I wouldn't mind investing in research on that subject, to prove you wrong," Howard said. "Maybe have a few people fill out a question-naire."

"Maybe. If people are willing to spend a few minutes answering questions for free," George said.

"I will prove you wrong right here," Howard turned to a woman walking into the coffee shop, "Excuse me, madam, would you mind participating in a research project by taking a couple of minutes to answer a few questions?"

"Nope! Running late for work, sorry!" The woman looked at her cellphone.

"Good try, Howard," George laughed.

"Any ideas?" Howard pulled out of his pocket an index card and a fine-point Bic pen. "George, what do you suggest we do?"

"It's simple Howard. We need the art to exhibit, the

place where to exhibit it, and the questionnaire for the visitors to fill out at the exit."

"We already have the art. This poster is fine," Howard pointed.

"No!" George slapped the table. "This poster would be the end of me as an appreciator of true art. Posters are designed for commercial purposes to hypnotize the masses, so people buy things like zombies."

"OK, got that down. Any ideas? Danae?"

"No!" George said and paused.

"What then, George?"

"We will display a live woman!"

"Live woman it is," Howard jotted down a note. "Now, if you don't mind me asking, where do we find a live woman?"

"Yeah, really, where do we find a live woman?" George pondered. "I see artists place advertisements in newspapers, 'looking for live models,' and such, maybe that would work."

"I will put an ad in the *Andover Daily News*," Howard noted on his index card, "What else?"

"I say, if we do anything, we do it like a real exhibition," George said.

"We need a gallery.... Rent a space," Howard wrote down.

"When I think about it, I would prefer a more natural environment."

"Park?"

"Maybe! But I feel a more intimate natural environment would be better."

"Like in a garden or something?" Howard asked.

"Yes, like a garden," George agreed. "In fact, we can use my garden across the street. More precisely, we can use my gazebo, although it would need to be remodeled a little to make it suitable for the demands of the display."

"George, you'll be the manager of the project," Howard announced.

"No, Howard!" George held up his palm. "I am a happily retired art teacher. Einstein said that creativity is a product of idleness, and I love idleness. Let me tell you, Howard, this is the kind of lifestyle I would not give up for any…"

"$40 thousand per year!" Howard interrupted.

"No, Howard," George insisted, "It's not about the money…"

"$65 thousand, and paid vacation."

"Deal," George slapped the table.

"You do your thing, George," Howard finished his coffee, pulled a linen handkerchief out of his pocket, and delicately touched the corners of his mouth. "I will be the money! I will write the checks. I am good at that, I practiced my whole life." He folded the handkerchief neatly and put it back in his pocket.

"Howard, just out of curiosity, why would you want to invest in this?"

"To prove you wrong, George," Howard leaned across the table and paused. "But mostly for fun. You see, business investment is like magic. You think you are doing it, but actually it is doing itself. It has a nature of its own. I like to watch it evolve into…. into… whatever it wants, really."

THREE

At 5 p.m. sharp I finished my meditation and ran out on the street to meet Martin. The red CRV showed from behind the curve and pulled by the curb. I hopped on the seat, wrapped my arms around Martin, and leaned my head on his shoulder. Except for a deep sigh, he was silent as he drove half a mile to the apartment complex. We got out of the car and stepped onto the narrow path towards our staircase, I skipped in front of Martin, so we walked up the narrow stairs single file.

"What is that, Marie?"

"Where?" I was startled.

"On the back of your leg," Martin bent to take a look as I stepped on the stairs. "Jesus! You have dilated telangiectasia, Marie!"

"What is it? Is it a bug?" I screamed.

"No, not a bug. Worse!" he said pointing at the back of my leg.

I twisted backwards to see what it was. "Oh, that! That's just a spider vein," I said, relieved.

"It is an offshoot of a bigger capillary."

"Perhaps. Don't worry, it appears only if I run, or stand for a prolonged period of time. It doesn't hurt," I ran up the stairs skipping a step to be faster.

"Doesn't hurt? And you don't mind that it's ugly? You don't mind that you look like an old woman?" Martin sounded shocked.

"It's on the back of my leg, I don't even see it."

"But I do."

"You do now, true."

"Now? I should not ever be exposed to such a thing."

"Okay, I agree. What do you recommend that I do? I don't know that there is anything I can do about it."

"Oh, yes you can!" Martin said, as we entered our apartment.

"Some sort of surgery?"

"Injection, not surgery. Sclerotherapy."

"Okay, I will google it."

"I'm surprised by your casual disregard of your bodily imperfections," Martin shook his head. He washed his hands, sat on the couch, turned on the TV, pulled out of his backpack a few scientific journals, picked up one and started reading, every now and then glancing at the news and switching channels during commercial breaks.

"Dinner is ready," I sang, and placed a Ball jar with daisies on the table.

"I do not want to look at you and eat my food, Marie. I want to look at the television," Martin said.

I stood motionless looking at the daisies. *In this light they look frozen*, I thought.

With bare fingers like my mother does, I extinguished the candle and placed some food on a plate and put the plate on the tray. I grabbed the Ball jar with daises, put it on the tray next to the turkey legs, and took the tray to the couch.

I sat at the dining table behind Martin and closed my eyes for a few minutes. Still the image of him sitting in front of me lingered in my awareness. Suddenly I felt how he must be feeling, striving to achieve something, to become somebody, and all by himself. Our life together blazed in front of me in a flash. How we met, how he wasn't sure I was the right person for him, how he went with Brigitte Bardot, how he got back to me, how he doubted we were a good match, how we got married in a courtroom.

"Marie, you are spiritual, I am materialistic. You are artistic, I am scientific. You believe in love, I believe in business," *he repeated so many times that finally I got it. I not only was convinced we would never get married, I thought we should be prohibited by law to get married. I embraced our relationship the way it was, content with the uncertainty and lack of clarity of what it was. Surrendering to the moment meant letting go of* *my dreams of romance, family, children.*

"Marie, I think we should get married on May 26," *he said, and called the courthouse. "I would like to book a civil marriage-act ceremony," he said.*

Civil or not civil, natural law is not in support, *I thought.*

When he came out of the bathroom that morning, perfectly beautiful, two bowls of raisin-wheat-bran cereal with fat-free milk were on the table. "Breakfast? What is this?" he resisted. "I'm not hungry."

"It will take us an hour to get downtown and find a parking space. The civil marriage doesn't start until eleven and who knows how long it will take," I explained.

I was surprised to see him eat, considering he said he wasn't hungry. I watched him take spoonful after spoonful carefully, as not to stain his clothes.

On our way to the car, he checked out my outfit, "Saffron orange."

Not knowing whether to take it as a compliment or a criticism, I shrugged, "Thank you," and smiled. The ride to the courthouse was quiet and in that sense solemn. The entire hour felt like the goddess of faith was spinning the spindle, and the threads could be seen through the car window shimmering in the morning sun. I could swear I saw birds lining up on them. Maybe because I heard them sing.

Finding parking at that time of the day was not easy. "We are going to be late," he became frustrated driving around looking for a spot. "And why did you make me eat the breakfast? Food increases peristalsis," he touched his stomach.

On my cell phone, I quickly googled 'peristalsis.' Okay, nothing serious, *I thought.*

Whether we made it on time or not was not my concern. I didn't think this marriage would happen. The odds seemed to be against us since we met. We may not find the parking space. If we do find a parking space, we may not find the building. If we find the building, we may not find room 305-J. And what if we take the elevator to the third floor and the elevator gets stuck?

I even wasn't sure that the marriage should happen under our predicament. I put love ahead of a piece of paper. I felt he was my husband regardless whether we got married or not. I adored him the way he was, every step of the way. The way he is overly organized to the point of minutia. The way he needs to be always ahead of time. The way he likes to be aware of his environment. The way he wants me to be fit. The way he com-

plained about how I looked and what I did. The way he was getting more and more anxious yet was determined to override hurdles on the way to our wedding.

"Here," he said, and the next moment we were parked and running towards a large building.

He looked at his notes, "Room 305-J," he confirmed, and the race started. We ran up and down the stairs, flew up and down in the super-fast elevator, we asked people walking by, but room 305-J could not be found, and our wedding was to start in two minutes.

"Okay, you take the hallway to the right, and I will take the hallway to the left. When you are done, stand in the central lobby and wave if you found it."

We split many times like that, and each time we stood in the central lobby looking for each other, shaking our heads "No."

Finally, he ran to me, grabbed my arm, and dragged me along as he raced downstairs and across the street into another building, and three floors up to the room 305-J, where couples waited to be married. We barged into the big room. They all looked at us as if we were marathon runners crossing the finish line. Our faces red and sweaty, our hair disheveled, my makeup smeared. A few people clapped. "You made it, man," I heard someone say.

We sat down, like nothing happened. I looked at him. He looked like a teenager who just got off a first roller-coaster ride.

"Marie and Martin, please step forward," a woman announced.

We looked at each other, surprised they didn't take us off the list, considering we were half an hour late.

"Come, come," Martin took my hand and led me urgently towards the front of the courtroom.

We stood in front of the judge. Martin held my hand in both of his hands, looked into my eyes and smiled. It was the warmth from that smile that took me through all these years and will take me through thousands more. It was the tenderness of his hands holding mine. He invested himself into this moment fully, wholeheartedly. My mother said life is like a mosaic of moments. For me, this single moment became a mosaic larger than life.

When I opened my eyes, Martin was eating the last bite of his turkey leg, audibly sucking on a bone while watching the Discovery Channel documentary on Bengal tigers. I stood behind him, pretending I was watching TV too, and when he finished eating, I hugged him from behind. "I love you," I whispered. He didn't move. I gave him a quick kiss on the cheek and picked up the tray.

I cleaned up the dishes, scrubbed the kitchen floor, then went to the bathroom, took a mirror and looked at my spider vein. *Barely noticeable*, I felt relieved, went to the bed, lay down and stared in the darkness.

The TV rumbled continuously in the living room, followed by silence, and just when I was drifting into sleep, I heard soft music and the voices of women sighing and moaning with pleasure.

The air was dry and cold. I grabbed my coat and threw it on top of the comforter and pulled the comforter over my head.

FOUR

Through the open balcony door I could hear chatter and light laughter. *Romantic love*, I thought, *thrives on memories. This laughter will get them through many stormy moments.*

I remembered hearing a young man call my name. *I turned around, he smiled and said, "I knew it was you." A wide creek polluted by car-factory paint in my memory flowed like a great river with moon reflections bouncing off the water like ping pong balls. I smiled back and squinted to see his face in the darkness. I walked a couple of steps towards him. How did he know it was me? I thought. I believed him, overtaken by a feeling of familiarity. As soon as my eyes met his, I saw my reflection.*

It is memory that connects people and keeps them together. Memory inspired all the decisions I made. I clearly saw myself make those few steps based on nothing else but a shimmer of unity.

I finished my morning meditation, and while still sitting on the floor listened to the murmur of the fountain in the yard. After a few minutes, I opened my eyes and looked through the balcony door out into the garden. A couple was sitting on the bench by the fountain, sharing a single ice cream cone, bursting into laughter between every lick. As if they had been apart for too long. Or perhaps they just met and fell in love at first sight.

The thud of the morning newspaper startled me. I ran out, picked up the paper and spread it flat on the dining room floor. I noticed the ads were the same as the day before. Just as I started to fold the paper to trash it, at the bottom of the page a new ad, framed in a bold black border, caught my eye.

"$100/hour. Attractive woman needed for research project on human behavior."

I got up and went to the hallway. In the tall mirror, I looked at my reflection from every angle. "Don't think so," I had to admit.

I heard my phone ring.

"Hi, Martin! How are you?"

"Do you really want to know?"

"Of course."

"The situation is getting more serious," he said in a quiet, secretive tone of voice.

"What's happening," I whispered back.

"They are giving me somebody else's cases to continue working on."

"Okay!"

"Do you know what that means, Marie?"

"They know how good you are."

"Don't be so naïve, Marie," Martin whispered. "They want me to take responsibility for someone else's shabby work."

"Oh."

"But I cannot take responsibility for someone else's work. So, either they are going to fire me for refusing to do it, or if they continue doing this to me I will quit, and we will be on welfare in no time. And that would be the end of my life, and you will have to take care of yourself."

"Maybe just tell them nicely that you do not feel you can work on other people's cases," I said.

"Nicely? You are funny. If I get to the point of telling them anything, I will be so upset, I will not be able to speak nicely, I guarantee you that. Got to run now."

"Okay, good luck. Love you," By the time I said 'love you,' he had already hung up, and I felt sad that I didn't say 'I love you' before I said 'good luck.' But he no doubt needed more good luck than my love at that moment.

I could hear him say, "Marie, your love is great, but we cannot buy food with it."

I walked around the house, head down, thinking. I stopped by the newspaper still spread on the floor. I fell down on my knees, I looked through the ads, desperate to find something. All I could see was "$100 per hour." Maybe because it was framed.

"I have no choice!" I whispered to myself as I dialed the number.

"Live Art Gallery," a male voice answered.

"I am interested in applying for the position for the research project," I said.

"OK," the male voice said. "Can you come tomorrow at 11 a.m.?"

"Yes. 1111 South Adams?"

"You got it."

FIVE

It was 10:30 a.m. and I was getting ready to go to my job appointment, the very first one since I decided to join the work force. I was so proud of myself that finally I would be qualified to talk from my personal experience about the difficulties of looking for a job and being rejected.

I put my backpack on and Googled the address, quickly realizing I would not be able to make it on time by foot. 1111 South Adams was in the opposite part of town. I thought of calling the office and rescheduling, but then I remembered Namaste and found his number in my phone.

"Namaste, Marie," he said right away.

"Do you still have that old van?" I asked.

"Yes! Right here in front of my garage."

"Is it running?"

"Short distances," he said.

"Can I borrow it?"

"Anytime! The key is on the passenger seat."

I jogged down the street a couple of blocks to Namaste's house. I saw the van parked in front of the garage. The windshield crack in the shape of a rising sun was still there since hippie days. Namaste said some people saw the sun setting, but he preferred to see it rising, so it stayed.

I got into the van and pulled the door, but the door didn't close. I tried harder, but the door still wouldn't close. I pulled with both hands and still nothing.

"Hi, Namaste," I called, "How do you close the door?"

"Slam it hard!"

"I did, but it isn't closing," I said.

"Lift a bit and slam at the same time."

"Okay, hold on, I will try." I used my last bit of energy and lifted and pulled and slammed, and it closed. "Thank you, Namaste," I hung up, ready to take off.

I grabbed the key from the seat and turned it on. The old engine rumbled for a few seconds and stopped. I tried again. *This is not going to work*, I thought and got my phone to cancel the interview. Before I was able to select the number, my phone rang.

"Give a couple of pushes on the gas pedal before you turn the key," Namaste said and hung up. I looked in the direction of his house and noticed a light movement of the window curtain.

I pushed the pedal two or three times and turned the key. The engine started rumbling and dark smoke came out of the exhaust pipe and enveloped the van as I backed onto the street.

SIX

I drove in circles through a residential area. Already 15 minutes late, I called the number from the paper.

"I have an 11 a.m. interview, but my GPS led me into a residential area," I said.

"South Adams, green house, look for the number 1111 above the red painted door."

I drove slowly and, a couple of houses down the road, I parked in front of the green house with the red door. The house was medium-sized with planters hanging off the eaves, surrounded with a well-trimmed juniper hedge. There was no sign that this could be a business.

This doesn't strike me as a research institute of any kind, I drummed my fingers on the steering wheel. "This cannot be good," I said out loud while dialing.

"Namaste, I am here for a job interview, but it's a residential area. It's a house not a business. There's no sign."

"People do business from their homes a lot these days. I give singing lessons at my house, right?"

"Right. Thank you," I said.

The street bathing in sunlight got hotter and hotter as

the clock moved towards noon. I felt a strong urge to turn around and go back home. Against the dusty windshield right above the rising-sun crack a faint outline of Martin's face emerged from the past, his big hazel eyes greener than normal.

"It is cold," he buttoned the top button of my coat, double wrapped my scarf around my neck and tied it into a knot under my chin. "There! Much better! Chili-Willi!" he kissed me on the nose and, as we walked into the snow-stormy street, he took my hand in his hand and put both our hands in his parka pocket. "Marie, you know what I want in this life. I have been clear. I want business, I want success, I want prosperity. What do you want?"

His hand holding mine felt so soft and warm, and our steps were in perfect synchrony as we strode down the street. "I want everything you want," I said.

"Okay," he smiled. "We will do it together."

"Yes, we will do it together," I agreed.

"Tell me, where do you see yourself in five years?"

"I see myself growing into a whole, balanced ..."

"But that is not the point," he interrupted. "That is a given. We are whole already. We are not broken. The question is, what are you going to do for money?"

"Go back to school..." I said hesitantly.

"Marie, how many times do I need to tell you? Studying literature will make you spend money. It will not increase your earning potential." His voice gained a notch in intensity with the last words, then softened again as he continued, "I need a business partner, a warrior who is going to fight on my side for a better future. Do you think you can be the one?" He looked at me askance and waited for my answer. I didn't know what to

say. All I could think was his hand holding mine in his pocket.

"Okay! Silence speaks better than words," he said with resignation. "If you are not part of the solution, you are a problem," he added.

The wind lashed frozen rain and snowflakes into our faces. By the time we arrived at the entrance door of the building where he worked, we were coated with ice. We stood there for a minute, looking at each other. With his hand, he brushed ice and snow from my hair, then took off his hat and put it on my head.

"To keep you warm," he said. "Sorry, Marie, you cannot help me," he said softly, apologetically, forgivingly, dismissingly. Then he smiled slightly with the corners of his mouth and stood for a few seconds like that. I didn't mind any of this. If he stayed there like that forever, I would not need to eat or sleep. I could have lived an eternal life just off the light of his being. But he had to go to work, so as soon as he glanced at his watch, he spread his arms wide, embraced me and kissed me on the forehead.

As my memory faded, the bitter taste of Martin's words "Sorry Marie, you cannot help me" strangled my heart.

I felt the cold van AC air blowing into my face. "No!" I said firmly, stepped out of the van and slammed the door so hard it closed without lifting.

As my hand poised to knock on the red painted door, the door opened.

"You found us!" a stout gentleman with thick gray hair and smile wrinkles around his eyes opened the door and briefly glanced at my body up and down.

As soon as I heard "us," I felt encouraged and peeked inside.

"Please come in," the man pushed the door wide open. I scanned the inside of the house fast, but saw no sign of a business setting, nor anyone else's presence, and hesitated for a moment.

"Come in please, have a seat," the man touched my elbow.

I resisted a strong urge to run out, and reluctantly sat on the chair closest to the door.

"This project is sponsored by a venture capitalist who wants to stay anonymous," the man said, stretching slightly his red suspenders with his thumbs.

"Piña Colada?" he got up.

"No thanks," I said.

He walked to the kitchen and came back carrying a glass of Piña Colada with a yellow umbrella on top.

"I would like to tell you a bit about the job," he sipped his drink. "We need a woman of considerably proportionate physique to participate in a behavioral study on why people like looking at women. The woman would need to feel comfortable being on display while lightly dressed."

"How lightly?" I asked.

"Bikini lightly," he said.

"Really?" I said. "It would have been nice if you mentioned that light detail in the ad."

He nodded and slurped his drink. "We wanted to talk the details in person." He looked into the glass. "A Raphael sky blue and rose bikini, the colors of eternity and the heart." His eyes misted. "These are the colors that have uplifted people for centuries."

"Very nice, but I may not be the right person."

34

"We are looking more for what I would call an artistic presentation."

"Aha," I said. "And where would she be presented?"

"Around here," he motioned with his arms.

"In your house?"

"House or yard, we are figuring out the details."

"I am not sure this form of art is for me, but thank you for your time," I said.

"No worries, we will be interviewing this week, then we will be considering all our options."

"So I guess I will go now," I got up.

"Thank you for coming," the gentleman got up and walked me to the door, "Do you have any last minute questions?"

"No, I got it." I waved my hand and walked the path between the bushes towards the street.

"Call me if you do," he shouted across the yard.

I waved to the man, "I won't."

I opened the van door and got in. "It looked good in the paper. Too good to be true," I mumbled.

I turned on the engine and turned up the AC. I dazed out looking down the street trembling in the heat of the air. I couldn't reflect back upon the experience. It felt like it never happened.

SEVEN

Driving home from the strange job interview, I couldn't bear the idea of being late to meet Martin at the curb. My entire life with him I was always early, waiting for him. When I think about it, it feels like our entire relationship rested on my ability to wait. Sometimes it was painful, but still, the best waiting ever. So truly waiting. Dry, empty, longing packed with hope and anxiety. Like walking thirsty through the desert, wherever you look, no sign of water. But hope blossoms on the barren land. In deserts lost travelers, do run into oases, fertile, fruitful, green and bountiful.

What if he doesn't appear? That killer question haunted me every step of the way, the knife in my back that I had no time to worry about. Like a wounded warrior, I kept waiting, bleeding out slowly, yet never giving up, and never going back home without him. And so, he always showed, except for our first date, but that was my mistake.

We had arranged to meet at the plaza where young people gathered every night. It was my first date ever, a month after my 26th birthday. I put on my white lacy top and my favorite skirt, white tiered with pink ribbons marking each level. I

36

walked in a more dignified way than usual. Like I came from a different world, feminine in the purest of ways. The world I used to suppress.

I led a solitary life, and to be surrounded with thousands of young people felt a bit overwhelming. It felt superficial on the level that it was a place to look for a partner. In my mind looking intentionally for a partner was embarrassing. In fact, I thought one does not look for a partner. God, destiny, Mother Nature does it. If and when it is supposed to happen, we find each other. Yet there I was, standing by the concrete bench by the rambling rose bush crumpled in a bunch, supported by nothing. Soon I was surrounded by young men, observing me as if I were an exhibit. Maybe because I had never been here before.

The area was discreetly lit, which made me a bit nervous. In truth, what made me very nervous was the fact that the clock on the square showed 8:05 p.m., which meant that Martin was 5 minutes late. Very soon he was 10 minutes late, and even sooner he was 15 minutes late, and in no time, I realized he is not coming. My heart was pounding so hard, I was afraid it might jump out of my open mouth gasping for air. Fear consumed me. The faint light on the plaza faded into total darkness.

By 9 p.m., the young people coupled up and left, and the street looked dark and desolate. I walked to the bus station. The bus was already there waiting for me with all doors wide open. I walked in, happy to see that except for the drunk looking old man sleeping on the floor in the back of the bus, I was alone and could be sad as much as I wanted.

To my mother's surprise, I walked straight through the house and into my room, sat on my bed, grabbed my mime ragdoll for consolation, and just when I allowed my tears to surface, I got startled by the ringing of the phone. Within a minute my *mother barged in holding the phone in one hand while silently pointing at it with another.*

"Hello," I said sniffling.

"Hi. What happened? I waited half an hour."

"I waited for an hour."

"Where?"

"By the concrete bench? Near the rose bush."

"When?"

"From eight till nine."

"We were supposed to meet at 7:30 p.m.!"

"Oh. Sorry."

"I can still come and pick you up, if you want."

"Sure," I threw my mime ragdoll on the bed, wiped off my tears, and ran out on the street to wait for Martin by the curb, leaving my mother standing in the middle of my room perplexed. I expected she would still be standing there when I came back.

Driving back home after my so-called job interview, I ran a few errands since I had the van. I kept looking at the clock every minute. *I can make it, I can make it,* I mumbled. I made a few stops getting some groceries, which wouldn't normally make me late. But with the farmers market going on, traffic was snail pacing. Drops of sweat felt like liquid cinders on my forehead.

"Where were you?" Martin said, already sitting on the couch watching TV.

"I got a few things for your sandwich," I hugged him with such force he moved his face away to protect his teeth.

"Any chocolates?" he struggled under my embrace.

"White and Black's almond milk." I stepped back, grabbed the chocolate quickly from the bag, and hid it behind my back.

"Where is it?" Martin rummaged through the bag.

"Here it is," I showed Martin my hand with the chocolate in it, and ran around the dining room.

"You trickster!" Martin chased me around the apartment for a few minutes, wrestled me down to the floor, and snatched the chocolate from my hands. We rolled on the floor laughing. Martin unwrapped the chocolate and offered it to me. I broke off a little piece, Martin ate the rest.

"It is so sad we cannot have children, Mousy, you would be such a good mom," he said, lying on the floor, chewing on a piece of chocolate.

"My clock is ticking," I looked at the ceiling fan rotating fast.

"Putting pressure on me isn't going to help," he said and sat up.

"Didn't mean to pressure you, just saying it might be a good time."

"And how are we going to support a child?" he asked.

"Children don't need much."

"We don't have a house, my job situation is not stable, and you are not in a position to contribute. Maybe God doesn't want us to have children." Martin sat on the couch and switched the channels.

I sat on the floor in front of him cross-legged. "My mom always says, 'God will provide.'"

"Then go ahead and marry that God who is going to provide. I am not him." Martin switched the channel.

I looked into Martin's eyes silently, then knelt on the floor and embraced him, my head on his shoulder. He leaned his head on top of mine for a few seconds and said gently, "OK, go now. I have so much to read."

"Do you know what a beautiful man you are?" I said, taking his head in my hands and scattering a few quick kisses over his face.

"What?" He said absentmindedly.

I got up and went to the kitchen. I cleaned the dishes, wiped the counter top, scrubbed the floor, dusted the blinds, and continued with the bathroom.

I scrubbed the bathtub sparkly clean and moved on to the sink. I sprayed Windex all over the mirror. As I wiped the mirror, I saw the clear reflection of myself, my dark hair in disarray, my tears as if frozen in the corners of my eyes. I locked the bathroom door, took off my clothes, and stood there only in my sports bra and briefs. I turned around slowly and looked at my image in the mirror from all sides. A knock on the bathroom door startled me.

"Marie, I need the bathroom! What are you doing in there for so long?"

"Just cleaning." I quickly put on my dress, reached for the doorknob, unlocked the door, immediately got on my knees and started wiping the floor tiles.

"Why did you lock?" he said.

"By mistake, I guess," I mumbled as I continued wiping on my way out.

EIGHT

I woke up early to see Martin off to work.

"Shall I make you a sandwich for lunch?" I asked.

"No, I will go to Subway next door," he said.

"Have a nice day, *carpe diem*," I wrapped my arms around him.

"*Carpe diem*," he saluted back, grabbed the doorknob and stood there thinking, his forehead almost resting against the wood door. I watched him turn around in slow motion facing me, looking at my face. It felt like he was going to communicate some profound truth of great importance, one that had been heavy on his soul for a very long time. One that could be said only once. And now was the time.

Then it seemed like he changed his mind. He vacillated. He struggled internally. His face turned from concerned to determined, as he put his right hand into his jacket pocket and pulled out his phone. He swept it open, selected an app and took a picture of me. Once I realized what was happening, I tried to smile but was sure I hadn't made a full smile in the rush. He shot fast.

He pulled up the photo, looked at it with resignation and turned the screen towards me. Yes, half a smile, and crooked too. One eye was half closed, so the other stared abnormally up. I must have blinked with one eye and looked up at Martin with the other.

"Your first-morning look," he announced. "What do you think?" he asked, tilting his head to the side to wait for my answer.

"Jesus Christ!" I whispered.

"Yep!" he nodded, turned on his heel, and went out.

I watched him glide light-footed down the stairs and, as soon as he disappeared, I ran across the living room onto the balcony, and watched him walk towards the parking lot. Tall and slim, he walked gracefully with his back straight, like someone who is strong and knows his strength.

He got into the red Honda CRV, turned on the engine, and took a minute to allow the car to warm up, adjusting the rearview mirror, the lateral mirrors, checking all the gauges and buttons, as it was his before-taking-off routine. I looked through the impeccably clean windshield into his focused face. "So pure," I whispered. I wasn't sure what it meant exactly. Just that he felt untouched by life. In spite of his strongly voiced desire to live fully, he elegantly avoided gripping life, expecting that somehow life should embrace him in a favorable way. He was not versed in life the way other people are. Other people attack life, and wrestle life into submission. He engages in a mystical no-touch, light-and-shadow dance with life.

I waited for a few minutes after Martin disappeared down the road, then grabbed my phone and ran to the mirror. I fixed my hair and took a selfie.

"Ha! Not bad at all!" I said to my image in the mirror, then forwarded the picture to Martin. "Look, much better!"

I typed the message and shot the send arrow. I placed a call.

"Namaste! Good morning,"

"Namaste!"

"Thank you for letting me borrow your van."

"The van is available for anyone to use. The key is always on the seat," he said.

"That is good to know. I might need it. But I am not certain."

"Uncertainty is the reality, that's certain," he said.

"How do we become certain?" I asked.

"We don't," he said.

"So we stay uncertain?"

"Certainly."

"Namaste."

"Namaste."

I didn't understand what he meant but didn't have time to pursue it and selected another number from my contacts.

"Good morning."

"Good morning, Marie."

"I am sorry I do not remember that I ever heard your name," I said.

"It is George, George Harris."

"George, is that position still open?"

"Yes. We narrowed down our choices but have not made the final decision yet."

"I would like to consider it."

"I'll put you back on the list. I will call you for the costume rehearsal."

"Thank you," I said.

Costume rehearsal? I thought. *May God help me*, I rolled my eyes.

NINE

"How did it go George? Do we have a woman?" Howard sipped his coffee.

"Let me tell you Howard, this I could never have imagined in my wildest dreams," George slurped his macchiato. "Hundreds of applicants flooded to my house. Fleshy, thin, pretty face, bold, timid, you name it."

"You are aware of the fact that any man in your position would be quite thrilled."

"Yes, men who like the circus. But not me! This is a business project for my art, and I was trying not to get too excited with the superficial presentations I was witnessing. I selected three, and even that was a stretch. 'Wear your bikini under your clothes, we will be having a view, ok?' I told them. 'You are going to like this,' one of them shook her behind. 'And you are going to like these,' the other shook her breasts. This is the worst of Hollywood that I ever witnessed. Now do you still believe you are paying me enough?"

"Ha, ha, ha!" Howard laughed. "$65,000 per year, with two weeks paid vacation? In addition to being in the company of some fine ladies? Most of the male species would have paid *me* for a job like that?" Howard touched the corners of his mouth with a monogrammed handkerchief. "You said there were three of them?"

"The third one had a unique demeanor. She didn't seem to think she was there to display the parts of her body. Yet she had quite a distinct shape that retained a certain innocence as it developed and molded itself."

"Oh!? So, are you thinking what I am thinking you are thinking?"

"I think I am thinking what you think I am thinking," George dipped a biscotti into his macchiato. "I told her, 'My idea is new to me and new to you. How it works we'll find out as we move forward.' I pointed out the window, 'Do you see the gazebo? It's 50 feet back from the sidewalk. You will be displayed like on a stage, standing with your arms outstretched. Your hands will be comfortably secured to opposite posts of the gazebo. Not too tight, not too loose. You will be standing for two hours each day, completely open to viewers,' I explained to her."

"What did she say?" Howard leaned forward.

"'Will I be standing outside in winter in my bikini?' she asked. I said, 'In bad weather, we'll move the exhibit inside, you'll be standing in my big bay window, over there, arms stretched out just like in the gazebo. We don't miss a day! Six days every week.'"

"What did she say?" Howard asked.

"Nothing. She just watched with wide open eyes and said nothing."

"What else did *you* say?"

"I reassured her, 'This is art. I'll never touch you. No one will ever touch you.'"

"So, she is going to do it!?"
George bit on a piece of biscotti, "I don't know."

TEN

"My plan requires a sign, a gazebo, that woman Marie I hope she's reliable, a tall fence in back, and a short fence in front," George talked to himself looking around the sofa for his cellphone. "And a cash register!" he added, bursting into quick laughter.

"Hadley, I need you!" he said into his phone. "Got a new project! Woman in a bikini installed where people can look at her! I need a sign in the front yard that reads 'Live Art Gallery.' I need your gazebo more open in the front."

"George, my friend!" Hadley said.

"When can you come?"

"I've got a furnace to install today, including a new 220 line! Tomorrow, I install a bathtub — a big 72-inch soaker — with a new drain and faucets. Then, can you believe it, the mayor wants a gazebo just like yours! That's what he said, 'Just like George's.' It'll be next week before I get to you."

"Next week? But I'm ready now!" George insisted. "Put the mayor off, see? I've got a plan!"

"Ha, ha!" chuckled Hadley. "You want everything right

now, just like a fussy baby! Let's say Friday, this week, 8:00 a.m."

"Okay, Hadley! You're the boss. You'll modify the gazebo first, and I'll explain about the sign. You'll know what to do."

"Yes, George, you tell me what to do, and then I will know what to do. See you Friday!"

George mused and murmured, "Hadley's lined up. That gives me four days to shore up my six-foot back fence and my four-foot front fence. Need to draft the questionnaire too."

The floor of the gazebo rose four feet above ground. On Friday, Hadley completely removed the gazebo's front fence units and the step railings. An unobstructed view ran from the floor to the ceiling of the gazebo, and from one side to the other where the woman's wrists would be secured. "Every inch of the woman will face the front, open and stretched out," George explained.

Hadley installed an oversized sign that read LIVE ART GALLERY.

"Are you sure, George?" he motioned with his head towards the sign.

"I don't want any question about that. My idea does not involve sex!" George hectored. "My plan is not pornography! No way, José! The woman in her bikini outside in the gazebo and the bikini exhibits inside my house are ART! It isn't even nudity! All the pictures, all of them! All the sculptures, videos, and installations are bikini-themed! Every one of them! This gallery is art! The woman is art! Live art!"

Hadley put his tools back in a five-gallon bucket. "No doubt you are confident, George. Pure art!" he winked. "If you don't mind, I'll just check with Pastor Greg about that."

"What?" George jerked his suspenders. "Pastor Greg! What are you talking about?"

"You know, for my own peace of mind, I would prefer not to rot in Hell!" Hadley pulled out a pad and pencil. "Let's settle up the bill."

"Right. Come on in the house." George gestured.

ELEVEN

George felt warm and content walking around his new gallery with paintings and photographs of women in bikinis on the walls. Large and small statues of women in bikinis adorned pedestals and tables throughout the room. Screens mounted on the walls featured successions of still photos and videos showing bikini-clad maidens. "Most women come and go in the world at large, but these ladies stay with me for a lifetime. This is art, my collection of art!" He stretched his suspenders.

"Good morning, Daisy," he greeted a chubby one with rosy cheeks dressed in a bikini style from the fifties.

"How do you do, my lady?" he bowed to another.

"And how are you, Rose? As beautiful as ever, my dear! Beauty is truth. Truth beauty! Ha! As someone wisely said. Now for the scientific survey!" he announced. His yellow pencil in hand, George sat on the inner edge of the big bay window behind the life-size manikin wearing a lacy bikini and began to write.

CONFIDENTIAL GALLERY QUESTIONNAIRE

Thank you for taking a few minutes to answer these questions.

1. Why are you here? _____

2. What do you experience when you view the exhibit? _____

_____

3. What attracts you to come here? _____

4. What is the most attractive aspect of this exhibit? _____

5. Did this display impact you in any way? If yes, describe. _____

_____

6. How many times have you visited this exhibit? _____

7. Comments and suggestions: _____

_____

Thank you from the Live Art Gallery Management

Just as George finished drafting the questionnaire, Howard marched through the front door carrying a huge fruit basket wrapped in cellophane tied with a silver ribbon. "Howard, you are the greatest!" George exclaimed. "I feel just like a navel orange!"

"George! Take a navel orange. Take two! Take three!" He looked around George's living room. "What happened here? What are all these photos and paintings and statues and videos? What's going on?"

George unwrapped the cellophane and grabbed a plump, heavy navel orange. He began to peel it. "My lawyer, the great Frank Master, says we need an art gallery to give credibility to the live-art display."

Howard pursed his lips and squinted. "Frank probably saved me millions right there!"

George swept his hand in a flourish and thrust a piece of paper at Howard. "Here! Here's our scientific survey for the greater glory of live-art installations. This is our roadmap to grants and ever-widening public acceptance!"

Howard stepped back from George's attack on the orange and studied the questionnaire.

"Yummy! Juicy and sweet, Howard! Like all these ladies in the gallery!"

"George, my friend, my artist friend nonpareil, this is indeed a great questionnaire. When we have a thousand of these, we'll have our scientific database."

"Then all my labors of love for art, and lots and lots of your financial backing, and the woman's long hours in the gazebo will enhance the achievements of artists and scientists alike. We will have answered the question we first asked at the DailyFix, when we saw the big poster that attracted so much attention!"

"You recall that poster didn't do anything for *me*," Howard said.

"You are a major exception, somehow, Howard."

"Pure, George, pure, but not puritanical."

"Now, tell me, what about these questions? Do you have anything to add?"

"Add? George, I'm adding $65,000 to your bank account, how about that? You taught art for forty years. You know how to ask questions about art. You live art. You breathe art. I live money. I breathe money. Go with your gut feeling!"

TWELVE

"You are going to have some problems, George! Problems. Lots of problems, as your lawyer, I'm obliged to let you know," Frank said looking at the gazebo.

"Why? Because I want to make my contribution to art? And to science alike?"

"You're going to need me, maybe more than once."

"It's art, Frank!"

"Will the fundamentalist ministers think it's art?"

"God knows it is art. God will forgive me."

"Will Pastor Colfax and his narrow-minded flock think it's art? Will they forgive you? It's a naked woman, restrained, for God's sake!" The lawyer paused. He tilted his head back and mocked, "Oh-h-h, it's a terrible, sinful snare for the innocent! *Res ipsa loquitur!*"

"She's not naked! You're one of my best friends, don't you see what I'm saying?"

"Will the mayor think it's art when the masses converge on his office demanding an end to obscenity — your exhibition — in Andover?"

"Publications are obscene. This is not a publication. It's an artistic installation!" George said.

"Zealots, the righteous! Ah, George, sometimes they miss these subtle distinctions! Sometimes these zealots get confused."

"Cooler heads will prevail!" said George.

"You wish! What about the police and the sheriff? Now, that's the meat of the coconut! If they miss your subtle distinction about art, in this case, if they misconstrue the law in favor of their famous knee-jerk reactions, then *you* pay for their mistakes! Oh, you will pay!"

"Yes, yes. You may be right. I have anticipated that. It's in the budget. You may have to defend something like that in court."

"That's for sure!" said the lawyer. "But what about the media, George?"

"I'm glad you remembered the media, Frank! They'll be here in force! Color photographs on page one of the newspaper. Local evening news on television, etcetera! To me, that's publicity for my art installation! That's not a problem. People will come from everywhere to see the woman standing in the gazebo! Oh, the throngs! The rich and the poor! Art on a grand scale!"

"Children!" Frank interjected. "What if children come?"

"Young and old! Beautiful and plain! They'll all come! Welcome to live art!" George motioned theatrically with his arms wide open.

"George, you are right!" The lawyer smiled.

"And the greatest result will be when many, many viewers of my novel live-art installation report their thoughts and feelings about why they, why each individual is powerfully attracted to view the woman in the bikini! Psychologists and sociologists will eat it up!"

"George, it's science," chirped Frank, with a grin on his face, adding "*vel non*."

"You must come, Frank. Our grand opening is on Tuesday, four days from today!"

THIRTEEN

I ran to the van a few blocks down the street, jumped on the seat, lifted and slammed the door, pushed the gas pedal a couple of times and turned on the engine. I drove to the first mall down the road, purchased a red bikini for what George called "the rehearsal," whatever that meant, and headed for South Adams.

"Marie, let's take a walk," George said.

My phone buzzed, but I didn't look.

The remodeled gazebo stood empty and quiet. A slightly elevated platform in the middle awaited the art.

"It is for you to stand on," George said proudly.

"I see."

It looked very simple. Not much to behold. The air around the gazebo, the emptiness of space, the suspense and expectation it evoked, carried a certain undefined power, mellowed by the rambling rose in full bloom.

"And the research subjects will be walking around." George motioned with his arms.

"What are the silver rings for?" I pointed.

"Your arms will be outstretched and tied with ropes to

each of these rings" he explained.

I looked around the platform and looked at the structure. I felt the energy of the vortex in the middle of the pedestal and the empty rings awaiting my hands. "I am not sure I can do it, George," I said, and grabbed my buzzing phone from the purse. "Excuse me for a second," I said and glanced at the text: "Marie, I'm so distressed. Ready to give up on my profession and my life."

For a second, the gazebo and George faded away. When the noise of alarms in my head subsided, I felt an urgency to text back, but wasn't sure what to say.

"The rings should give some slack," George flipped the rings up and down to demonstrate.

"George, excuse me for a second. I need to send a text." I looked at my phone. "Let's talk when you come back home. Love you," I texted Martin, feeling how what I said was a painfully weak reply bringing me no relief.

"The research subjects are scheduled to come in 15 minutes." George pulled at his LIVE ART baseball cap. "Let's try this one session and see how you feel."

I didn't expect to start today and wasn't ready. "I guess that would be fair," suddenly I heard myself agree.

I went to the restroom to change. I came out and noticed George tilting his head and looking at my body up and down.

"Do I just stand here?" I asked.

"Yes, and I'll put these leather bracelets on your wrists." He pulled them out of his pocket. "Touch, they're padded."

I touched the bracelet. "Soft," I said.

"Now we will secure the bracelets on your wrists with ropes to the posts," George threaded thick ropes, the kind I only imagined on big ships.

"For how long?" I asked.

"Two hours. It will always be two hours, noon to 2:00 p.m. Just today, our first test run is 2:30 to 4:30 p.m., starting now."

I stepped to the center of the gazebo. George tied my hands straight out to the rings on the posts then swirled the leftover rope on the floor around me and to the side, as an artistic arrangement. He stepped back and checked his creation.

"Hey, George," a gentleman called from a short distance away. George moved to him and they talked for a while. Then they stepped in front of me and gave me a good look.

"This will work, George. Where do they do the paperwork?" I heard him say.

"As they exit the gate, the box with questionnaires is on the right side. See the arrow pointing at it?" George motioned.

"Great, I will be the first one then, you know, for good luck," the gentleman said.

"I should have gotten champagne, Howard."

"Piña Colada will do, George."

As soon as the older gentleman left, a slow steady flow of viewers paraded in front of me. Each of them looked at me as they walked along the sidewalk outside the fence. Once the research subjects started flowing, I struggled to shut down my feelings.

This didn't feel the best line of work for me. It felt I was doing something that was not productive, and might even be useless. The world around us is to be appreciated and enjoyed, and me standing in the gazebo should be considered okay. Yet, there could be an element of doing associated with standing that I may not be able to do. Am I supposed to be appealing, or sexually attractive, or just me?

I grew up thinking that being dressed in a provocative way isn't fair. Seduction assumes intentionally acting in a certain way, which appears to be false and manipulative. Anyone can dress lightly and most likely it would create an intended effect. I didn't believe that a connection between two people should be based on seduction.

Unless I was joking, I don't remember playing any such kind of a game. Rather than artificially enhancing my physical beauty, more often than not, I tried to underplay and diminish it.

"You are 26 years old, why are you dressing like a twelve-year-old girl?" Martin said a few weeks after we met. "Do you expect I should find you sexually attractive? I'm not interested in children."

"How should I dress?" I asked.

"I don't know, tighter and shorter skirt outlining your form, perhaps. More revealing tops, some make up…. And tan for God's sake; pale skin is unattractive. You are a woman; you should know how to sexually attract a man."

I was a woman who believed sexual attraction is based on the attraction of souls. And since Martin and I already were attracted that way naturally, at least I hoped so, I was ready to do whatever he desired and went shopping.

Short tight leather skirt, high heels, see-through lacy top, full make-up. I looked in the mirror and couldn't recognize myself. When I stepped out of my room, my mother was startled, "Excuse me," she ran after me and touched my shoulder, "Whom are you looking for?"

When I saw Martin, he didn't recognize me either. "You?!

Let me see! I cannot believe it! You actually did it." He was *entertained alright, but I didn't believe he loved me more just because I put on such a different kind of garb.*

The excitement about my costume subsided quickly. I looked at Martin and quietly debated whether to ask or not. "How was your weekend?" I finally asked.

"Fantastic!" he smiled. "We drove to Chicago, stayed in a hotel by the lake, and did water sports. Pedal boats, kayaking, swimming, water skiing, you name it. We did it all! Doug did his seal impersonations, and I laughed so hard I fell into the lake. Claire and Sonya jumped after and raced me to the shore. My classmates are so much fun, good sense of humor..."

Martin sounded so genuinely happy. I don't remember seeing him so thrilled. Tears came down my face, and they were black.

"Why are you crying?" He asked.

"Just testing my mascara, it's supposed to be waterproof."

"Busted!" he laughed, and I felt grateful I was able to make him laugh

Technically speaking, I can do anything, I thought, standing at the gazebo for the first time. Just that I was supposed to do nothing. George believed in me from the first moment, and for no apparent reason, which was my favorite thing.

Appealing perhaps I could somehow be, and that would be in synchrony with my ethical and psychological makeup to the degree I'm naturally capable of being. If I'm supposed to evoke an erotic interest, then whatever I am doing, which is basically nothing, and whoever I am, which I'm figuring out, will be exuding that erotic quality naturally, or not.

To evoke sexual desire was a premise most foreign to

me, since it is so much on the level of action, and for me to act that way would be devoid of being genuinely evocative. Even if I could act, I doubted anyone would be affected by it. I felt like the only way to do this would be to mold this presentation into something that is suitable to who I felt I was at every given moment. To be like a statue that morphs itself on the outside, based solely on a genuine feeling from inside.

The more physically tired I felt standing in the gazebo, the more my thoughts, memories and feelings faded into nothing. After two hours my arms and legs felt as if made of wood, and when George released my wrists, I sat down on the stage to rub my body for a few minutes.

"How do you feel?" George asked.

"Standing is difficult and my arms hurt, but otherwise it is easier than I expected," I summarized, doubting that what I said was a hundred percent accurate.

"Here is your $200 check. Let me know if you are planning on coming tomorrow."

George's question reminded me of the feeling Martin's text from two hours ago stirred. It was still there inside my heart, throbbing for attention.

"I'll be here, George!"

I dressed, went to the van and happily slammed the door hard. I sat for a while. The sun settled behind the Wild Bear Bank skyscraper far in the distant downtown area. The tree shadows stretched thin, ready to disappear into the dusk. I looked at the clock, *almost five*. I pressed the gas pedal three times before turning the ignition on.

I dropped off the van and ran as fast as I could to meet Martin. Just when I turned into Hoover Avenue and barely could see the end of it where it curved to the left, I noticed the red Honda CRV. With my last breath of energy, I sprinted towards the car to meet him before he turned into the apartment complex, barely making it.

"Where you've been, Mousy?" Martin asked as soon as I jumped into the car.

I wrapped my arms around his neck, and he embraced me with his right arm as he drove with his left.

"You are sweating?" he said.

"Not normally," I rested my head on Martin's shoulder.

Martin said nothing about his work, and I didn't ask any questions. He was practical, and I had nothing significant to offer, so why probe the wound? The two-hundred-dollar check in my pocket made me feel like I was doing something to help, but deep inside I knew that $200 would not make any difference to Martin.

Later, when Martin finished his supper, I went to the bedroom to make a phone call.

"Namaste! Would you mind if I put your address on my new bank account?"

"Not at all. If they mail anything, I will put it in the van; you seem to be the only one using it. If you wish, you can keep the key, I have a spare one."

"Great! Namaste."

FOURTEEN

It took me a while to fall asleep. I had conflicting feelings about what I did today. It didn't seem natural to me, and certainly didn't feel artistic. Besides, I ate too much lasagna for dinner and I felt discomfort in my stomach.

As soon as I started falling asleep, the bedroom door opened, and for a second a wedge-shaped light split the darkness of the bedroom. Martin walked carefully to the bed and fully dressed lay down flat on his back on the top of the cover.

"Mousy, are you asleep?" he asked softly.

"No," I said.

"You are such a cute Mousy-Mouse, I want to be able to take care of you, you know," he sighed a deep, long sigh.

"What is it?" I turned to face him and put my arm across his chest.

"What 'what' is it?"

"You sighed."

"You don't expect me to be happy, do you?"

I certainly expected everyone to be happy, and especially Martin, but the tone of his question stopped me in my tracks, and I didn't know how to answer it.

"I don't think I will be able to succeed," he continued. "No matter how much I'm trying to distract myself, it is always on the back on my mind."

"Trust me Martin, you are the most capable man I've ever known."

"How many men have you known? Closely?"

"Closely? Maybe...."

"Two, three?" he interrupted. "And none of them ambitious," he shook his head.

"I guess they were in their own way."

"I am ambitious, Marie. And not in their way. I'm ambitious in my way. I don't want to waste my life on unimportant things." He lay there quietly. In the darkness, I could see him immersed in his inner thoughts. His face twitched as he tried to form words, and he whispered something to himself.

"Did you want to say something?" I asked.

"Did I want to say something? Are you trying to placate me? Of what use would it be to say something? So, you can hear me, understand me, and perhaps, God forbid, try to help me? But I am positive there is not a chance."

"I wouldn't..."

"Don't waste your words, Marie. I am alone in this life. I have no partner. I am dejected and lonely."

"I'm here. Look, I'm here," I spread my free arm to attract his attention in the dark.

"Sure you are, Marie, and you are nice, but you cannot live the kind of lifestyle I am interested in." He thought hard again, as he bit on his lower lip, and continued, "For example—and forgive me if I never expressed this before, my mind is overburdened with worries and I forget things easily—I am scientific, Marie, I believe in science. I don't believe in mumbo-jumbo voodoo. On the other hand, you believe in acupuncture. I saw our bank account. Cannot believe you spent thousands on useless acupuncture!"

"I did it for the baby."

"Why didn't you do science for the baby?"

"Because western medicine offers only in-vitro fertilization, which we cannot afford."

"As much as you would like to have children, you never did anything to afford them. Strange," he scratched his head. "You didn't do anything because you are not materialistically minded like me. You are spiritual. What I say to that is, first you have to afford it, then you can be spiritual as much as you want."

"Material and spiritual are not mutually exclusive."

"They are to me."

I closed my eyes and sank into such a deep silence I witnessed myself falling asleep.

"I would like to have a dog. Maybe two," he woke me up.

"They do allow smaller dogs in this apartment complex," I said.

"First of all, I want a big dog. Second, dogs need a yard. I would not like to have my dog confined within a one-bedroom apartment, which would be inhumane." Leaning on his bent elbow, he turned his upper body towards me. "You see how limited I am by my life," he whispered, "I cannot even have a dog and take my dog for a walk, like normal people do."

"We can go for a walk sometime like we used to," I said.

"Since you seem not to remember, let me remind you. Walking is an exercise for wimps. It burns a hundred calories per mile, but it takes twenty minutes to half an hour, and builds only hamstrings and gluts. Fat legs and a big butt are not aesthetic. A pear shape is not attractive. Besides walking is boring," Martin said. He lay on his back and folded his arms above his head. "Where was I?"

"You said you wanted to go for a walk with your dog."

"Yes, because I would have to. I cannot send the dog alone for a walk, can I?"

"No, of course not," I admitted. Under the faint street light sifting through the curtain, even half asleep, I could see he was thinking. His big shiny eyes focusing on the ceiling moved left and right, as if reading an invisible script written up there.

"Swimming is a bit better then walking. You are developing the upper body rather than the lower, and you are not sweating like a pig," he said.

"Down the road on University Street, there is an Olympic-size indoor swimming pool," I mumbled.

"You are crazy if you think I would get in my Speedos like this?"

"Like what?"

"I need to get in better shape to go swimming, but I don't expect you to understand that."

"No, I do understand. Of course," I petted his chest in slow and short strokes. "I was thinking, there is a gym there too. We can go to the gym and then swim after we get in shape."

"My method of exercising is scientific, and efficient. Pullups, pushups, and crunches. I can do it at home, I don't need to waste my time and money going to the gym. But I am concerned about you."

"Why?" My eyes opened wide.

"Your gastrocnemius muscles are too pronounced, that's why."

"Pronounced? Really? Is that why I have indigestion if I eat too much food?"

"You must be kidding me?"

"No, why?"

"I'm talking about your lower leg muscles. How is that related to your digestion?"

"I don't know, you said it."

"No, I didn't."

"Yes, you did," I said, dozing off.

"What did I say, Marie? Repeat."

"You said gastro ... something," I tried to remember.

"Gastrocnemius! That's your leg muscles, Mousie. You should stop running and walking, and I am yet to see you reach twelve pullups, which you promised me a long time ago. How many can you do? None!"

"Oh, no, no!" I protested. "I can do more than none for sure."

"How many more than none?"

"At least six."

"Yeah, cheating."

"Okay, two properly and four cheating."

"Why would you cheat on yourself? Pullups would make your arms stronger, and your abs more defined."

"That's goooood," I said fighting falling asleep.

"We need to get in shape, not only to look attractive, but to get strong physically and mentally. Life is a fight for survival, and we don't have parents to help us." His voice faded into the stillness of my sleep.

"What is your goal, Marie?"

"What?" I woke up.

"Where do you see yourself in five, ten years?"

I tried to think hard, but there was no way I could come up with an answer to that question with a fully awake brain, much less half asleep.

"Money," is all that I could mumble.

"Money what?"

"I want money," I felt like a Wall Street parrot with a sleep disorder.

"Everyone wants money, that is not an issue. But how do you plan to get money?"

I was aware of every second of falling asleep, and it felt like falling off a cliff in slow motion.

"Marie," Martin raised his voice, "are you asleep?"

"No!" I jerked myself into wakefulness.

"So why aren't you answering my question?"

"I am thinking..." Yes, I was thinking, trying hard to evoke what the question was. When I woke up enough, I knew I would have to say something, or he would be upset.

"I will write a book," I heard myself say. That woke me up completely. Am I out of my mind? Book? What would I write about? Except for a short poem which I wrote when I was nine and a literary essay on moon images in *Jane Eyre*, I hardly wrote anything else. I wasn't prepared to answer more specific questions. I struggled to create a gap in my mind to prevent Martin from pursuing the subject.

"That is not a bad idea," he said suddenly. "J.K. Rowling is making a fortune as we speak."

"You know she was on food stamps before she became

famous," I said, trying to divert the discussion from my nonexistent writing project.

"Well, we are almost on food stamps too, so that should work in your favor," he said. "The question is, what are we going to do until you become rich and famous?"

"We keep getting ready."

"I thought we have been keeping getting ready already. By now we should have gotten way too ready. I don't know if I can keep getting any readier any more. I am almost forty, and I am exhausted."

"We are there," I announced.

"I better see some signs of that soon. I am running out of time. I'm running out of my mind. I'm running out of life. My life is on hold, hanging by a thread," he said, got up and went to the living room.

FIFTEEN

The night was restless. My recurring baby dream came back full force.

"You left me," the baby said, crying loudly.

"No, I am here. I never left you."

"Yes, you did, you are a bad mother, bad mother...," the baby screamed.

"I am holding you in my arms...."

"Doesn't matter," the baby slapped me on the face.

"If I am holding you in my arms, then I am here and you are here," I said softly, feeling my face burn.

"You are here alright, but I am not because you left me behind," the baby screamed into my face and disappeared.

I screamed. The bedroom door opened and the light of the living room cut sharp into the darkness.

"Did you scream?" Martin stood like a dark shadow in the middle of the light.

"No, I didn't."

"Then who did?"

"I don't know. I was asleep."

"Did you have a bad dream?"

I thought for a second, "I think I did," I said, still surprised that such a tiny baby could have such a powerful voice.

Martin sat on the bed and hugged me. "It's just a dream, just random electrical brain impulses," he pulled me closer to him and held me tight. "You're shaking," he said.

"I'm cold, I think." He placed a blanket over the comforter.

George called first thing in the morning, "Marie, are we on for 12 noon?"

"George, can I put you on hold for a second?"

"Sure."

I paced the living room a few times, then stopped in front of the balcony door. I watched a woman walk along the path to the swimming pool with a bunch of kids. *How cute*, I thought. *All of them hers?* I wondered. Then I realized, she is dressed to swim. In her bikini. No big deal. After all, it is much easier to stand in the gazebo than to write a book. Especially when you have nothing to write about. Besides, writing a book is a riskier investment of my time. It is uncertain when and whether at all it will turn into income.

This is an emergency, I thought.

"George."

"Yes ma'am."

"I will be there at 12 noon."

Time is my only enemy. Always fighting for it or against it. It disappears while it lasts, like sand in an hour glass. When you look back you don't see time, you see only sand. The trace of time haunted me in my dreams and when awake. It is not about what it is, but what we perceive it to be. In my mind the memory of the past is everlasting, seamlessly woven into the present. I remembered to the point of manifesting, ever since I wrote my first poem.

I was nine. Our teacher took us to the fields to observe the changes in nature. We sat in the middle of a field with corn stubs spread in all directions to infinity. It was a warm October day, with the last taste of summer fading away fast.

"Children, look around!" our teacher said, her voice dissolving into space, as if she spoke to the wind.

We sat on the dry soil and looked. Perhaps for the first time, evoking seeing into our awareness. Till that moment I felt as if the world imposed seeing upon me. Things were there and therefore I saw them. That day I learned that I can look around and decide what I am seeing.

Smelling the scent of dry foliage, tasting the dust we stirred when we shuffled our feet against the ground like a herd of goats. I looked far away where the field met the sky. The air vibrating with existence, the corn stubs shining like gold coins lined upright across the field. The sound of a bird flying above our heads. The expansive ocean-deep-blue tone of the sky.

"What do you see?" the teacher asked.

Students raised their hands. "Sky," "Cloud," "Bird," they listed.

I sat small and silent, imbedded into the furrow, merging with the soil. "Marie, what do you see?" the teacher turned to me.

I looked far into the distance where the barren field splashed into the emptiness of the sky.

"I see the space."

"Is there anything in that space?"

"Nothing."

"Okay," the teacher nodded, "Nothing. How does it make you feel?"

I thought for a second. "Big," I said, and the entire class burst into laughter.

The birds gleaning bugs and leftover corn grains flew in bunches up in the air. The wind scattered the children's giggles over the field until it echoed back from all sides, and it felt like we were sitting inside a cave filled with laugher. The teacher waited for the class to calm down, but the laughter wasn't subsiding on its own.

"Quiet, please," the teacher shouted until silence regained its power across the field. "Now write a poem about what you see," she said.

Everyone looked down at their notebook pages flapping in the wind like white birds. I looked at mine and couldn't think. It was then that I realized that thinking is not as important as grown-ups thought it was. "Think Marie, think!" I heard my father say and felt my math notebook slap on my head. But sometimes you cannot think. Sometimes, the more they tell you to think, the more thoughtless you feel.

It was while I sat imbedded in that furrow that I realized that there are certain things for which thinking might not even be good. And even when we think we had thought things through, we still have to do the work. The work has a mind of its own and doesn't always align itself with the thought. Therefore, thinking is good for nothing.

Forget about thinking, *I thought, and felt the space float in my head. That felt natural. I watched my hand write a few lines and was thankful, for if I thought of it, I wouldn't have known what to say.*

"Who wants to share?" the teacher said.

Everyone read what they wrote. It was all about earth and the sky, which was pretty much all that there was. The words uttered by children flew up into the air, and dropped down, scattered like seeds over the field.

"Marie, what did you write?" I heard the teacher's voice. "Would you share with us, please?"

I really didn't want to share because I had nothing smart to write but felt I had to because I was asked to. Besides, everyone else shared their poems, and it would be only fair that I shared mine.

"Space is chasing a green horse
Green horse turns into space
There is no space nor horse
There is nothing to see
But a turning of thrones."

That day I will remember forever. For that day, though no one understood what I wrote, I became a poet. And although I never wrote a poem ever again, deep inside, I stayed a poet.

My English teacher said, "Poets are not poets for the way they write, but for the way they see."

"I saw nothing, and I became a poet," I said.

My teacher waited for the class to stop laughing. "Seeing inside your mind counts," she said.

SIXTEEN

At 12 noon, I was at the gazebo feeling the wind touching lightly my skin like a love song. Being enveloped by space was relaxing and humbling. Not so many people walked by, allowing for lots of silence. Silence felt like a deliberate act of waiting.

In small ways, I was always forced to practice waiting, the mastery of which evaded me consistently. Except maybe that one time when I stood from late afternoon till late night by the sidewalk under a small tree at the edge of a park. Waiting. Waiting for what appeared like a duration of many lifetimes.

It was a young weeping willow tree, with the supple branches cascading almost to the ground. I stood so close to its trunk I had the tree bark relief imprinted along my spine for months.

He said he would not want to see me anymore. He would be spending time with Donna. "She has a great sense of humor, she makes me laugh," he said. I hadn't seen him in a few weeks and thought to take a peek at him as he got off his work. I didn't want him to see me in my deep state of desperation, so I hid under the weeping willow on the edge of the park located diagonally from the entrance of the building where he worked. People walked on the sidewalk by the weeping willow without noticing that I was there, so I believed he would not notice me either.

I merged with the branches and made a little hole in them through which to spy on the building entrance. The leaves were delicately green, smelling of sap. Each time the building door opened I was shaken by an expectation anxiety.

At first the door opened and shut frequently, then less and less and less. On the second floor where he worked, I could see the lights being turned on, and some people walking back and forth. Eventually, the busy building turned into a deserted place like a cardboard table-top display of a building that once was there. Soon, all the windows were lit with yellow light. The noise of vacuum cleaners could be heard across the plaza. A few women carried buckets outside, put them by the door, and hurriedly mopped the stairs. Quickly, as if not to be noticed, they went inside, and soon all the lights turned off, and no one exited through that door again.

The emptiness spread everywhere and felt eerie. I pulled deeper into the tree. Ready to wait forever, determined never to leave this leafy embrace. As I watched all the lights switch off, deep inside I felt blank. Blank was all that there was. And the blank was gold. By being nothing, it potentially could turn into anything. I stared into the blank space inside for a long time. Then I saw the shiny seeds everywhere, sprouting into hope. Suddenly, the full blast of hope hit me.

Hope stirred me to consider climbing the tree to take a broader view. He must be somewhere. I looked up. It was too small a tree to climb without breaking branches and falling down, so I just stood there listening to white noise murmuring *from the leaves. Gradually, the murmur became louder and louder. I looked around. The sidewalk glistened under the street lights. Rain, I thought. The drops of rain grew in size and strength and bounced off the leaves and branches with fast increasing power.*

A few scattered passersby ran for shelter in a nearby bar. Then the streets became empty. The plaza turned into a Seur-at-style painting. Full of dots. I waited until the last inch of my dress became drenched, took off my shoes and walked to the bus station barefoot.

The memory faded, and I found myself standing in the gazebo on a perfect sunny day, happy to see George walking towards the gazebo to untie my hands. *That was easy,* I thought, feeling that this job would be a great opportunity to perfect waiting. There was a long road ahead of me. But from now on it was going to be easy like a song. A lyric came to my head, as I drove back home. "Your love is easy, eeeasy like a sooong. Oh yeah, your love is eeeasy...," I sang to myself all the way to Namaste's house. I parked the van and ran for my life.

Martin pulled by the curb. I sat on the passenger seat and wrapped my arms around his neck.

"Look, look!" he shook my arm and pointed at a woman running on the sidewalk.

"See her muscles, she is body building," he said. "Why can't you look like her?"

"I could," I said.

"Then why don't you?" he asked.

"I cannot lift weights."

"Why, what's wrong with you?"

"Nothing is wrong with me. The weights are too heavy."

"Well, that's a good thing. Resistance. If I were a woman, that is how I would like to look. Muscle definition is sexy."

"It's nice."

"Are you mocking me, Mousy Mouse?"

"No, no. I am agreeing."

"So why don't you exercise?"

"I do…"

"No, you don't!" he said. "Yoga is not exercising."

SEVENTEEN

"Happy birthday to you! Happy birthday to you!" ..., my mom sang on the speakerphone.

"Thanks mom," I rolled the cookie dough into small balls and placed them on the cookie sheet.

"Marie, you are 37, I cannot believe it!"

"Why cannot you believe? You know when you gave me birth. Who will believe it if you don't, mom?"

"I mean, what are you waiting for?"

"What do you mean?"

"What do I mean? I mean it is time for you to have a child."

"Martin is not ready to be a father."

"No one is ever ready to be a father. They become ready on the spot, the moment they see the baby. That is how it is preordained by God."

"I believe you, mom," With my index finger, I quickly imprinted dents into each dough-ball.

"Marie, listen to me now, you know I dealt with infertility myself...."

"Mom, I am not dealing with infertility." I looked on the shelf at my assortment of jam jars.

"Not yet," mom said sternly.

"I'll cross that road when I get to it."

"It's in front of you, Marie. You have to cross it now!" Mom paused.

"Mom, is it raspberry or strawberry jam that you use for thumb-print cookies?" I looked at the jars reflecting numerous shades of colors, from orange to burgundy.

"It doesn't matter, Marie! You know anything works," she said. "I'm talking here important stuff," she sighed, "Where was I?"

"Crossing the road," I reminded her.

"Yes. So, first thing you find a good infertility doctor...."

"No, mom! Why? I haven't even tried to get pregnant."

"It is a routine thing for women after thirty-five, that's why. Especially since you've been married for a while now, and you never got accidentally pregnant. Even if you are using protection, still it should have happened. It happens all the time." She paused for a second. "You are not on the pill, are you?"

"No," I scooped a spoonful of strawberry jam.

"Any other method of protection? Diaphragm? Disrupted coitus?"

"Mom! Please!"

"What?"

"It's too personal."

"All right!" she said quietly. "I'm just trying to help."

With a butter knife, I allocated a small amount of jam into each dent on the top of each cookie.

"Marie!"

"Yes?"

"How often do you have sexual intercourse?"

"What! Really, mom?"

I looked at the cookie sheet, blooming red with perfectly lined up cookies, six rows, four in each row.

"You don't even have sex, do you?"

I slid the cookie sheet in the oven and slammed the door. "Marie?"

I washed my hands and dried them with a kitchen towel. "Mom, thank you for the kitchen towels," I said. "They come in handy."

"Okay! You don't," mom said. "Still you need to see an infertility expert."

"They are so soft...."

"Unusual," mom said.

"No, kitchen towels are supposed to be soft."

"Who cares about kitchen towels, Marie!" she yelled. "When was the last time?"

"Five years ago."

"Double unusual."

"Usual or unusual, I love the man."

"Triple unusual."

I checked the cookies, although it had been only a few minutes since I put them in. They hadn't even gotten warm.

"Men are easy to seduce. You have to try something."

"Like what?"

"Like everything you think might turn him on." She got quiet. "What does turn him on?"

"I don't know. He says he likes tanned women."

"That's easy. Tan. More?"

"He likes perfectly shaved women."

"Shave for God's sake, Marie. Shave your head if necessary. More?"

"Porn movies."

"Then watch porn with him. Learn pole dancing, learn synchronized swimming. Whatever. And fast."

"Artificial methods of seduction are not my expertise. Isn't he supposed to find me attractive the way I am?"

"No, he is not. No man is."

"Thank you, mom," I said.

"Now get to it. Age waits for no one."

"I know. And no one has ever defeated Father Time," I mocked.

I felt enlightened in a certain way, yet some burden rested on my shoulders. I checked the cookies. The red jam on the top sizzling, although the dough was still white, untouched by the heat.

EIGHTEEN

"Marie, before you get to your position I wanted to talk for a few minutes," George said, as soon as I changed into my bikini.

"What is it, George?" I said.

"Based on requests coming from the research subjects, the sponsor of this project suggested that we give an opportunity to everyone to sit within the fence in front of you, so that they get to be in a closer proximity. Some of them said that walking on the sidewalk doesn't give them enough perspective to discern what they feel."

"I noticed some of them come often," I said.

"They are the ones who petitioned we give them permission to come inside the fence. We decided to charge an admission," George said and paused, looking at me. "And of course, that would mean extra pay for you."

"Oh."

"Think about it, and let me know," he said.

"Okay."

"Break a leg."

"Standing there tied to the posts?"

George laughed and walked away.

"Hey, George," I called after him. "How much more?"

"$10 per research subject inside the fence."

"Deal!"

George kept walking away. "Hey, George, you going to tie my wrists, or what?"

He scurried back and tied my outstretched arms.

Doing this for a while made me more and more confident, but this time the nervousness came back. Standing there, I felt fidgety in my attempt to find a comfortable position. As people passed by so close to me, or sat in lawn chairs, I found myself posing in a more pronounced way, and even smiling slightly, the way cover-page stars do. I felt I was turning into someone I was not, or perhaps was, but didn't know till now.

George stood by the gate watching the scene as manager of the project. I saw him talking with passersby and people sitting within the fence. I felt safe with George being there. He was a gentle fatherly figure. Protective, but not overpowering. Always smiling and encouraging, clapping his hands like a giant, good-natured seal.

"Hey everyone, over here by the gate," he clapped a few times. "I will collect the entrance fee, then you walk along the path to our art display in the gazebo. Enjoy, and don't forget to fill out the questionnaire at the end, look over there." He clapped again and pointed, "There is an arrow on the box. Come back again, we love seeing you here. This is a revolutionary approach to art. You will become part of contemporary art history books."

As more and more people took advantage of chairs placed inside the fence closer to the gazebo, I felt the invasive feeling transforming into a more comfortable feeling towards the closeness of strangers. I saw no alternative.

A few of the visitors spent quite a lot of time sitting and watching me, and once I exhausted my feeling of discomfort, I myself started observing the observers, looking into their faces or glancing at them in passing, and thinking, *what are they gaining from this? What are they running from? Where are they going to? Is this bringing any comfort to their daily struggles?*

I realized that my body became more fluid as I shifted from one leg to the other. The few times my mouth relaxed into a smile, the onlookers smiled back at me. In those moments, I felt my heart melting into this new feeling that we were in this together, and that I was not isolated, because now they were closer.

What had seemed embarrassing, necessary work became a valuable exploration of what human closeness means. For the first time, after months of work, I left the gazebo stage with the feeling that I had done something meaningful. I felt good about myself. And this feeling of value had nothing to do with the money I received.

It is true that as I saw several people seated in front of me, my first thought was of Martin's practice and the amount of money accumulating in my account, which was for him. But that feeling faded away every time I glanced into people's eyes. There I saw simple human desires for connection. I felt their curiosity, their appreciation, even got a sense of what their story might be, and the entire project felt right.

An old lady, probably ninety years of age, barely shuffled along with her walker. A net bag filled with bread and onions dangled from the walker frame. She hobbled slowly to a stop. She pinched off the end of the bread, put it in her mouth, and sucked on it, looking at me.

"Oh, my dear, when I was your age, I was just as beautiful as you are." Out of her toothless mouth, along with a few crumbs of bread, an ancient voice came, feeble but unbroken. "Oh, I was drop-dead gorgeous. I can see it right in front of my eyes, the way I was, with a red rose in my hair."

She stared at me as if looking through me far beyond the gazebo, and the back fence, and roses. "I was every bit as gorgeous as you are. I can see myself on the beach at St. Tropez, pure as a newborn, my body firm, my skin tight, glowing like a fresh magnolia flower in the summer sun." Her eyes returned from long ago to me. "I would trade places with you in this moment. All these boys drooling over you would be drooling over me. I would make them laugh, make them happy! I know how to tickle their imagination, yes sirree. They'd be screaming for me! I'd be just standing, watching them. I would move my hips a little and wink." She demonstrated.

With my lips, I blew her a kiss, but she didn't see it. She was gone far back into her past. With her weak eyesight, her vision of sixty years ago was clearer than me standing in front of her. *God is kind*, I thought. *Let us stick to what brought us joy.*

"Oh, when I was young, oh, when I was irresistible, I was happy like rabbits in spring..." she shook her head as she pushed her walker and shuffled away.

Soon George came to untie my wrists. "A few people have expressed interest in meeting you and speaking with you," he said. "However, at this point, I thought I could speak with them about the research project and spare you the trouble, unless you think otherwise."

"You talk to them, George," I said. "You know what to say."

"That's what I thought. You are art, not entertainment."

At home, I unlocked the door and peeked inside. The TV was on. Martin was sitting on the couch, his knees spread, his elbows on his knees, holding the widely spread pages of the *Andover Daily News*.

I got on all fours and crawled towards Martin and snuck between his legs under the paper and continued crawling over his chest until I wrapped my arms around his neck and lay my head on his shoulder.

"It is you, Mousy," he laughed. "Go, go, go, I have things to read."

NINETEEN

"Look at this babe in cut-offs, Dan!" A middle-aged, beer-belly man nudged his buddy and pointed with his head in the direction of a Hollywood-pretty blond girl.

"Jeez, Bobby, how about that balcony?" Dan said, watching the young girl stroll arm in arm with her handsome young man.

"Hello, mama!" another man whispered, looking at the girl's legs as she passed by.

Looking at me, the young man said to his girlfriend, "Now there is an object of art!"

"Object?" the young lady jabbed him in the ribs. "She's a complete person with a full life!"

"Which doesn't make her less a piece of art."

"I'll bet she's making a ton of money."

"She deserves it."

"What do you mean 'she deserves it'? I could do that!" the girl pointed at me.

"Whatever," said the young man, and silently scanned my skin. "No tattoos," he said.

"Do you think she's prettier than me?" the young girl asked.

"She may be. Her face is classic, with chiseled features, like a statue, you know. Like Rodin or classical Greek, perhaps Venus de Milo. Her breasts are not larger than yours, her solar plexus is harder, her waist the same, her hips fuller, her arms and legs show stronger musculature, not soft like yours." He pinched her bicep and looked into his lady's eyes. "But prettier? She's not prettier than you. Nobody's prettier than you, with your radiant skin, hooded brown eyes, high cheekbones and long jawline, and your smiling lips. You're prettier than she is, face and body, but she's a hundred times more attractive — harder, with those muscles that want to play dangerous games, and wide-apart eyes that see everything. She's all player. She's built to play. She wants to play."

"*I* want to play!" the young lady gently slapped her boyfriend's face and pushed her breasts against him. Bobby and Dan watched attentively, as she put her arm around her boyfriend's waist and pinched his nipple. "Play that!" she mocked.

Bobby poked Dan with his elbow, "This art thing is better than I thought."

"Yep, dude, play that," Dan said with a smirk.

"Nope, he ain't gonna. He's a softy," Bobby said

"Go dude! What the hell?" Dan said watching the young man breath in deeply, looking at Marie. "I'm telling you Bobby, young people aren't what they used to be."

The young girlfriend lifted her bare leg into the young man's crotch.

"Young girls are better than ever," Dan mumbled with his mouth wide open.

The young man's face flushed as blood sped through his veins. His girlfriend moved against him, front on front, her nipples pushing sideways, her mound pressed against his. She wrapped her body around him like a sleeping bag, her hips moving side to side, caressing him.

With the corner of her eye, she caught him still looking at me. "Is that bondage?" she asked.

"Nah, that's art," he said.

"But her hands are bound to the posts."

Still excited, the young man straightened up and scrutinized me. "If it really was bondage, she might have a gag in her mouth. Her mouth might be taped shut. She might be blindfolded. The point is she would be restrained so that she couldn't move. Her legs might be spread apart with an ankle bar. She might be hit with a stick or whip or an electric-shock wand. If it was bondage, she'd be completely naked. This is not bondage. This is art," the young man concluded.

"Maybe we could try it," suggested the young lady. Their eyes met, moving towards the same page. "We could try it?"

"You mean art? Like the woman there?"

"No. Bondage, like you described." Her body flinched. She moved her head side to side, so the small silver feathers in her hair swept away from her face.

"You want some of that?"

"No. I want to do it to *you*, Charlie. Just what you said!"

"You want to tie me up so I can't move?"

"Then I can do anything I want to you, Charlie!"

"Oh my God, you're beautiful when you flush. What are we doing here?"

He took her hand hard, and they strode away in long, quick steps, as Bobby and Dan, and the entire crowd reluctantly shifted their focus back to me standing in the gazebo.

TWENTY

Unless I was running late rushing to meet Martin, driving back home had a sort of therapeutic value. Today, although the engine was screeching like a she-devil, I felt deep silence inside. Like in the near-death experience stories, I am moving through streets flooded with light in slow motion, in spite of the speed. I observed cars and people passing by oblivious of me. *Another realm*, I thought, *not something I was unfamiliar with. Life has many different layers, and each layer has its own truth, its own reality. Every event is another arabesque that gives deeper meaning to the choreography of life.*

When we first met, Martin's work place was on my way home if I chose that particular route. Which often I did. And whenever I did, I wondered how is it possible that the building I never noticed before, could so suddenly possess such magnetism? Tall square structure, simple architecture, with a touch of renaissance. From the moment I learned he worked there it became impossible to pass without being swallowed by the big gaping doors. I would go in and stand by his office door waiting. People were getting in and out, while I stood like an abandoned island. A feeling of autonomy of the soul untouched by anguish transcended the physical body.

"*You?!*" his assistant distinguished me from the wall against which I was pasted. "*Come in,*" she ordered.

"*I can wait until break,*" my mouth barely moved.

"*Now,*" she pulled me towards the door. "*Today, we work through our break,*" she pushed me hard into his office.

I stumbled inside and bumped into him standing by the water dispenser. "*You,*" he said evenly, matter-of-factly, as he failed to balance the cup of water in his hand.

I was always intrigued how he could say something without the slightest modulation in his tone of voice. It made me not know how to feel. Was it a pleasant surprise, or a polite way of saying "you again"?

"*Look what you did!*" he said and stared at the wet spot on his shirt.

"*Sorry,*" I brushed his shirt with my palm, and seeing that the soft fabric absorbed the water and that it would be impossible to brush it off, I grabbed napkins from the stand, and pressed them against his shirt to soak up some moisture.

"*Don't! You are making it worse,*" he pushed me away. "*It's fine, it will dry. Just that you have to be more careful. You might hurt someone barging in like that.*"

I stood there, crumpling the wet napkins in my hands.

"*I am busy here,*" he said and pointed at his desk by the window.

I looked through the window facing the façade of the building across the street. "*Okay, I'll go now,*" I said, but couldn't get myself going.

"*Did you want anything?*"

I wanted to say, "*I wanted to see you,*" but instead I just kept looking through the window.

"What do you want? Fast! I have to go." He snapped his fingers.

"Wanted to see if you would like to take ballroom dance class with me," I suddenly said, and pointed at the big sign on the building across the street clearly visible through the window: DANZA ITALIAN SCHOOL OF DANCE—LEARN BALLROOM. EVERY NIGHT 7–9 PM.

"Oh, I don't know, I don't have…"

"I'll pay for you!" I said fast.

"Okay."

"See you tonight, across the street."

Over the course of time, I surrendered to the humiliation and humbleness that I experienced in my relationship to Martin. I wanted to believe the divine often is characterized with these qualities. At the same time, I developed a variety of creative ways to see him, perhaps one more time before it all was over. These little triumphs which flooded my heart with joy never lasted long enough.

How we dance with each other reflects how connected our souls are, *I thought. The very first time we danced together, which was a few days after we met, was smooth. Our bodies flowed in complete synch, moving as if guided by divine grace. We both knew it. We looked at each other and smiled. That was the memory my expectations were based upon.*

"Marie, what are you doing?" he paused dancing at the Danza that night.

"Dancing," I said.

"You don't know how!"

"I learned the Vienna Waltz when I was ten years old."

"You learned it wrong."

"Let's try again."

We tried for a couple of minutes.

"What are you doing?" He stopped.

One of the dance instructors stepped in, "What's going on here?"

"She hasn't got her steps right," Martin explained.

"Okay. Go ahead and try again," the instructor said and watched us dance. "Something is off," he said. "Let me see, Martin, what you are doing," he danced for a few minutes with Martin.

"Marie, now you," he danced with me. "Okay, I got it. You both know how to dance, just that Martin is taller and makes longer steps. So, Martin, you make shorter steps, and Marie, you make longer steps, and you will be just fine. Go ahead."

We danced while the instructor watched our every step nodding his head, content like a good parent who figured out how to manage his children.

I was looking forward to our next class with nervous energy. It's being in love, I justified the stomach jitters.

I was thrilled to see his car on the curb in front of my mother's house. I ran happily towards the door, jumped onto the passenger seat and wrapped my arms around his shoulders.

"How are you? Let me see. I love your hair," he said glancing at me as he drove.

He parked by the Danza studio, and I got out of the car and waited.

"Marie!" I heard his voice from the car. "I need to talk to you," He spoke through the open window. "Come in," he motioned.

I got back in the car next to him. "I came to tell you I will not be attending the dance class tonight," he said.

"Why?" I sighed.

He smiled and looked aside, "Greg wanted to introduce me to a few girls who expressed interest to meet me. I thought, why not?"

My mind and body turned into a stone statue for a few seconds. "Marie, I will not marry you," I remembered him saying the day after we had sex for the first time. "I am twenty-five, never been in a relationship, I do not know what I am looking for in a woman. I wouldn't mind continuing having sex with you once in a while, but I am interested in seeing other women. Can you do that?"

My heart was full of love and love understands, and appreciates, and accepts. "Yes, I can do that," I was confident. "Thank you for being honest. So few people are," I appreciated.

Now, sitting with him in the car, hit with the heavy dose of reality I created for myself, I thought how arrogant I had been to think that he will fall in love with me, and will not want to see anyone else. How manipulative I was to try to trick him into spending time with me, believing that the more time he spent with me the less time he will have to meet someone else. Now I am paying for that. There was a power of pride in strength that I felt at that moment, and that glimpse of pride made me flinch. I will have to pay for that too. Suddenly I felt sad for myself. Why should I suffer because I love? Isn't love a good thing? I don't want to blame myself for anything. I had no one to blame but love itself. But I would not blame my love.

He gave me a few minutes to process everything, "You go and dance. I will see you next time, I guess," he said.

"No! I will go home."

"Why don't you go dance with other men?"

"I am going home," I said, got out of the car, slammed the door, and ran down the street.

"Come in, I will drop you off," he called, and stopped by the curb near me.

I got back in the car. We said not a word. There were no words to be said. Words don't matter. Dance does. Or the lack of it. Like that time his father's friend's daughter Brigitte Bardot was visiting from Chicago and we went out to dance with Ben.

"Martin, can I dance with Marie?" Ben asked.

"Sure." Martin looked surprised by the question.

After a few dances we all gathered together.

"Donna, may I dance with you?" Ben asked.

"Sure," Donna looked at Martin for approval.

"Martin, you dance with Marie," Ben said.

"I don't want to dance with Marie," Martin said.

We all stood silently, as if the crystal ceiling was cracked. Ben looked at me and shrugged, 'Sorry, it cannot be pasted back together,' and swirled Donna onto the dance floor. Somewhere, at the edge of the universe, my feet felt cemented to the floor, and my heart was frozen. It was difficult to understand why Martin wouldn't dance with me, so I didn't try. Maybe because of that, the feeling of rejection pulled me down fast like a drowning stone. I tumbled into the void. Embarrassment and sadness immobilized my body and shut down my mind. Something had gotten obliterated inside of me. My soul faded to a blank point, like a snapshot of a moment in time, speaking louder than words.

Words often fail us. Memories fade. Pictures, which when moved in a sequence, make reality dance. *Like waves on the top of the ocean*, I thought, and parked by Namaste's house. Through the open window, I heard a female voice singing, and saw the curtain fluttering in the draft.

TWENTY-ONE

A uniformed policeman screeched his motorcycle to a halt and dismounted. "What's going on here?" he growled at the crowd on the sidewalk.

A middle-aged African-American looked up at the big policeman. "I'm just standing here on the sidewalk, Officer." The policeman silently glowered. "I was just leaving," the man scuttled away.

"Go on home! I don't want to see you around here!" the policeman barked after the man. He studied the crowd on the sidewalk. "You with the briefcase, come here!" he summoned with his index finger.

The man in the beige suit, with the blue and brown necktie, didn't budge. "Come over here, Officer. I want you to see what I see."

The officer walked to the man. "What's going on here?"

"That!" said the suit, pointing at Marie.

"Uh! Oh!" said the big cop. "Uh! Oh!" His eyes opened wide. "Obscene!" he said through his teeth. "This is the most-obscene picture I've seen in years! Somebody's going to jail! Who's in charge here?" he growled, and took several photographs. "I said, who's in charge here?" he shouted.

George stepped forward, face-to-face with the policeman. "Who are you?"

"Officer Everett Ready, Badge Number Five Five Eight, sir! You are in violation of the law!" he said.

"Officer, allow me to introduce myself. I am George Harris, proprietor of the Live Art Gallery. What you are looking at is our permanent installation, something of interest to many in our community. You are welcome here. I want to know what you think about our live art. Be sure to fill out the questionnaire at the exit," he pointed.

"I don't know about all that," the policeman said. "What I see is obscene. She's tied up, see? It's porno!"

"Not porn at all, Officer. Nor obscene neither. Just a piece of artwork, to gather the attention of spectators like yourself." George spoke smooth, directly, without hesitation, in his strong, clear voice. "What do you think, seriously?

"O-b-s-c-e-n-e," the big policeman spelled the word. "Not a problem, Mister...?" He pulled out his citation pad. "What's your name?"

"Harris, George Harris. This is my gallery, and she works for me."

"Not a problem, Mister Harris. I'll issue a citation, so nobody goes to jail right off."

"A citation for an installation that is clearly artistic?" asked George.

"Obscenity in Public." Officer Ready spoke aloud word-for-word as he wrote on his pad. "Displaying a woman in a public place within the city in a state of obscene exposure of her person, to wit, in an orange bikini standing with her arms stretched out and secured to two sides of a raised gazebo, in full frontal public view."

He handed the citation to George. "You show up Friday morning at 9:00 a.m. in Courtroom 2, at the courthouse. You should know better. Educated, wealthy man like you. You should know better."

George folded the citation and slid it into an inner pocket of his sport jacket. "What's your name again, Officer?" he asked.

"Officer Everett Ready, Badge Number Five Five Eight."

"Very good, Officer Ready. Will you be there in court on Friday morning?"

"With bells on!" chuckled the big cop, got on his motorcycle, and roared away down the street.

"And guess what? Frank will be ringing them!" declared George.

TWENTY-TWO

Friday morning, the accused defendant George Harris and his lawyer Frank Master walked into Courtroom 2. "Frank, this installation is art, plus for that matter, with the questionnaire, it's science. There's nothing obscene about Marie in my gazebo!"

"I understand, George. Let me do the talking, okay?"

"Sure, Frank. You know what to say."

"No kidding, George!"

Court was not yet in session. In a corner near the door, a police officer spoke sharply, "Doc, send them to jail!"

George nudged Frank, "That's the policeman who issued the citation!"

Frank turned around, "And that's the prosecutor talking to him."

"Ever, why have you done this to me?" the prosecutor protested.

"Done what? I showed you the photograph. There she is, strung out, practically naked!" the policeman replied.

"You charged the owner with obscenity!"

"Right!" The officer smiled.

"You may be very wrong, my friend," the prosecutor frowned. "It occurred in a public place?"

"It sure did."

"She was completely nude?"

"Wearing a bikini, next to nothing."

"Not even nude, Ever. Was she fornicating with anybody?"

"No."

"Was she flashing her breasts?"

"No."

"Covered by the bikini?"

"Yes."

"At all times?"

"At all times."

"Was she mooning anybody?"

"No."

"Was she engaged in any kind of sexual conduct whatsoever?"

"No."

"Was she playing with herself?"

"No."

"Are you sure?"

"Sure, I'm sure. I watched like a hawk for any inappropriate behavior, Doc."

"Was she dancing in a lewd way?"

"No."

"Did the defendant George Harris have an art gallery there?"

"Yes."

"Was there a sign?"

"Yes, a big sign."

"What did the sign say?"

"Live Art Gallery."

"Did the owner describe what the girl was doing?"

"He said she was an artistic installation."

"Sort of living art?"

"She was alive alright."

"Was she conversing with spectators?"

"Not while I was there."

"Tell me again, what made you think that conduct was chargeable as obscenity?"

"Nearly naked woman, standing up secured by her wrists to opposite posts of the gazebo. See, it's in the photograph!"

"Nothing sexual happening at all, was there, officer?"

"Listen, Doc, she didn't do anything or say anything sexual. But between you and me, as soon as I saw her, I knew right off she appealed to my prurient interest! That's obscenity!"

"Officer, let me advise you, she *does not* appeal to *my* prurient interest! She will *not* appeal to the judge's prurient interest, either! You are out of line here. The judge will laugh at you!"

"Prosecute them anyway, Doc! Make them defend against the charge. Punish the girl!"

"Ever, don't tell me what to do! There's no obscenity here. We've got to get rid of this case. I'm not presenting it to this judge in any way except as a dismissed charge! I ask you again, why did you do this to me?"

"Gee, Doc, I mean, I got excited right off!"

"So what? That's not a crime!"

The policeman hesitated, then blurted, "Doc, these bikini girls are evil. They will excite you and hurt you!"

"What are you talking about, Ever? Something I don't know here?"

"It's personal, Doc."

"Well, keep it to yourself! I don't need you around here anymore. You can go now. I'll take care of this. Go on!"

The prosecutor noticed Frank Master listening. "Frank, do you represent defendant Harris on this obscenity charge?"

"Good morning, Doc." Frank Master purred. "I'd like you to meet the defendant George Harris. He runs an art gallery here in town. Salt of the earth!"

"Save it, Frank. I've got to dismiss this case. Do you agree to dismissal?"

"Sure, sure. Total victory for the falsely accused!" He smiled at George, who smiled back. "Why are you jumping to dismiss it, Doc?"

"There's no obscenity here. The officer showed me a photograph of the display."

"I was just going to tell the judge the same thing!" Frank said.

"We don't enforce overzealous officers' knee-jerk reactions in my practice."

"Smart," Frank said.

"Right!" said the prosecutor, "The case is dismissed. Just sit on the back row. I'll bring your case up first, stating we've agreed to dismissal. The court will rule the case dismissed, and you can leave with the certainty of closure."

"Very good, Doc. We'll be seeing you."

"On behalf of the state, Mr. Harris, I apologize for the inconvenience."

"Very well, sir," answered George. "I have said straight

through it's an artistic installation, and scientific too, if you count the questionnaire."

"See you, Frank!" the prosecutor said, narrowing his eyes at George. He strode towards the judge's bench, just as the judge entered the room.

TWENTY-THREE

"Your dinner is ready." I handed the tray to Martin.

Martin ate his sandwich while watching the evening news. I sat at the table and took a few bites watching Martin. *He looks so boyish when he's focused, such a good man, a sweetheart.* A surge of love flooded my heart. I took my plate and sat on the floor by Martin's feet, leaning my back against the couch.

"Any good news on TV today?" I playfully pushed my shoulder against his leg.

"No *good* news," he said without diverting his eyes from the screen.

"There must be something goo...."

"Shhh," he pushed against the side of my body with his leg, "I want to hear this."

I ate slowly my steamed string beans, looking at each string getting smaller and smaller as it disappeared into my mouth. When I finished, still holding onto my empty plate, I looked at the pine tree outside by the balcony door, the light reflecting against the needles and a grayish hue enveloping drooping branches.

"Now you can talk, during the commercials," Martin looked down at me, "Mousy Mouse."

"How much money does it take to start a practice?"

"A lot."

"How much is a lot?"

"A quarter of a million to begin with."

"I guess you would first find a space…," I started.

"Yes, then have a company set up the equipment."

"Which co…."

"Shhh, the news is back," he said. He raised his palm.

I tried to calculate in my head how long I would need to work at $100/hour, plus the extras, two hours a day, six days a week, in order to get $250,000, but couldn't figure it out. The television noise and the fear that I might not be able to accomplish it, made it difficult to think. I got up and cleaned the dishes, then took my laptop to the bathroom, sat on the floor, and logged into my bank account.

"Barely twenty thousand," I whispered.

Disillusioned with the prospects of succeeding on my mission to help Martin, I went to the bedroom, lay down and tried to sleep. I could hear late night shows going on for a while. Laughter, cheering, applause. And just when I was drifting into sleep, I could hear the sighs and noises women make when they are experiencing pleasure.

I got up and opened the bedroom door quietly, but the hinges squeaked. I heard the click as the TV screen turned off. And then silence.

"What do you need?" Martin turned towards me.

"Nothing," I answered.

"Go back to bed, Marie, it's late."

TWENTY-FOUR

"What on Earth is this thing Guido you are taking me to?" An older, stout woman held onto her husband's arm.

"Live art, Sofia, I told you hundred times!"

"It better come before we die."

"Don't speak like that, Sofia. We are not even eighty, why would we die?"

"We been walking forever in this heat, Guido!"

"Because you are snail pacing, Sofia. The place is just couple of blocks down from our house."

"I am just saying that this better be worthy of my coming down in this heat. You dragged me here against my wish."

"Sofia, I said I will go alone, but you wouldn't let me."

"I don't want to worry about you, Guido. I don't know if this live art is like live tiger, or snake, or who knows what. I don't want to become a widow before my time."

"There is no danger, Sofia, how many times do I need to say?"

"No danger? Didn't you say just the other day a dog bit off someone's nose?"

"It isn't like that. They said on television it is…"

"I hate television!" she interrupted.

"Sofia, why would you hate television, you watch it all the time?"

"They lie on television Guido, I do not trust a word they say."

"You saw the news; they can't lie on the news."

"Why would this be on the news? Did someone die of a heart attack coming here?"

"No. What heart attack has to do with anything?"

"It has to do with me, I may not make it, Guido," she slowed down. "But if you make it alone, you will marry a young, more beautiful woman before the assigned mourning period is over, and you will not be sad for me at all." She stopped walking and burst into tears.

"Don't say that, Sofia," he whispered patting her back and looking around at people passing by. "It is this heat, you know, she's fine," he said to a woman watching them, and whispered to Sofia, "Honey, we are almost there."

"That's what you said an hour ago." She blew her nose into a handkerchief, jammed it into her dress pocket, and started walking fast angrily.

"Sofia, I said let's take the car, and you didn't want me to drive," Guido hurried up behind her.

"You told me it is in the neighborhood." She turned around and looked at Guido. "Besides, you drive like a maniac, I didn't want you to run over Gregorio."

"Gregorio? Who is Gregorio?"

"Our neighbor's cat. You don't know nothing!"

"Calm down, I would never run over Gregorio, Honey!"

"Don't you 'Honey' me no more! You are the one who said your glasses are no good."

"I didn't say they are no good! I said, 'I see double.'"

"That is great, Guido! But you can't tell which image is real."

"I can tell everything, Sofia, I always can, my eyes are like new, I can see like a falcon," he said, squinting at the wall with the sign LIVE ART GALLERY. "Here we are, I told you it is close."

"All I am saying is, it better be a masterpiece after all this...."

"Yes, ma'am, a genuine masterpiece of live art! Art for the ages! Thank you," George said, as he took their money.

They merged with the file inching through the gate and into the yard.

"You see, Sofia, over there," he pointed, "under the gazebo."

"Where?"

"See? Where people are gathering."

"Wait!" she stopped and opened her little purse, pulled out another white handkerchief and wiped the sweat off her red face. "'Rain,' they said on TV? They have no idea, I told you that!" She slapped his wrist.

"Do you see now?" Guido poked his head from behind the crowd.

"Can't see a damn thing," she said.

"It is coming to your right, Honey."

"How does it look, Guido?" She fished in her purse for her glasses.

"It ... it looks like a person," Guido answered.

She put on her glasses and moved to the right in front of Guido to take a look, "Oh, is that what that is?"

"You will see better in a minute, Honey, when we come

closer," Guido said cheerfully.

"I don't need to come closer to see that that women is naked!"

"She isn't, Honey...." Guido squinted towards the gazebo to make sure.

"Live art, my ass! This is live porn! I am not going. I am not a weirdo!" She crossed her arms.

"OK," he agreed. "You can wait over there under the tree, in the shade," he pointed.

"Are you out of your mind?" she screamed.

"No, just..." he mumbled.

"You think I would let you go sniff around that bitch?"

"No, no she is..."

"Don't tell me what she is," Sofia interrupted. "I see what she is. A prostitute! I bet this is what she does during the day, and at night she receives clients!"

"Come on, don't say that," he patted her on the back.

"You see a pretty young something, and right away you are defending her, you understand her better than me," she covered her face with the handkerchief and moaned softly, "Oh-h-h." Guido hugged her in support, and they moved forward with the crowd.

Guido stopped, "Honey, we are here," he announced.

Sofia stopped, removed the handkerchief from her face and spit in the direction of the gazebo. "Whore!" she said through her teeth.

"No, Honey, this is just the display," Guido explained.

"The display of a whore for men to come and lust after and spend money on! ... Children and wives hungry at home, and they are spending their last hundred dollars on a woman like this?"

The crowd gathered around the couple.

"This is live art, Sofia," Guido said softly, pointing at Marie as if he were curator of an art museum.

"Call me crazy, but I prefer dead art," she stamped her foot. "I like Mona Lisa. She is dead."

"Look, Honey, she has a bikini on," Guido squinted in Marie's direction. "And..."

"And you are shameless.... Old man lusting after a young woman like that!"

"No, I am not lusting! I am just looking," Guido explained.

"And why are you looking?"

"Because it is beautiful.... You see a beautiful thing, you look."

"Not if it is a despicable naked thing ... a vampire that sucks men's blood!" She hissed in Marie's direction. "I know you find other women more beautiful than me!" She hit him on the chest.

"No, no, not like that ... more like a piece of art." Guido started walking her slowly away from the gazebo, still squinting every now and then towards Marie.

"Piece of art my ass! This is a piece of porn. It isn't enough they have naked pictures everywhere, they have to have a real one naked."

"Is she really naked, Honey?" Guido stopped, turned around and gave Marie a good look.

"Enough of this circus!" Sofia swung her purse at him.

"Stop, stop, Sofia!" Guido covered his head with his arms, under which he took another long glance at Marie.

"Enough, mister, we are going home," she pulled on his arm.

"OK, home it is," he agreed, smiling as he looked backwards in the direction of the gazebo.

TWENTY-FIVE

Standing in the gazebo made me feel I was watching segments of life in its numerous aspects. I often felt that visitors were enshrined in gazebos of their own, and that the observation and appreciation was mutual.

"What is she doing, Mom?" I heard a little girl ask her mother.

"She is being a piece of art, Honey," the mother answered.

"Was she naughty?" the girl asked.

"No, Honey!"

"Then why is she tied up to the posts?"

"It is just for pretend," the mother explained.

"But Mom, it looks for real."

I had plenty of time to think about things people say and watch how the words of strangers affected me. I examined the most delicate feelings and listened to the faintest voices inside myself but at the end of the day I heard nothing to suggest that what we as people do is different than who we are, and who we are is the same. *That's how by knowing ourselves we know others*, it dawned on me.

Standing here dressed in my rose and pale blue bikini,

with my arms tied to opposite posts of the gazebo, wasn't for pretend. This piece of art that I am is real. The pain in my arm muscles is real, the tightness of my abdomen, the tension in my tendons, the skin burning in the early afternoon sun, the sweat tickling down my sternum—the itch I cannot scratch, the wind blowing my hair into my face. I am live art. We all are.

Existing in these moments of truth is the best part of my day. Memories come not as thoughts, but more as vivid scenes from a movie seen long ago. Tears come out of the joy of surrendering to the expansive space of the yard and the depth of perspective into which the street in front of me merges.

What if Martin finds out? I often thought about it, but not while at the gazebo. At the gazebo, I live art. This material world is suspended in a certain level of abstraction. Things lack clear lines of separation. Colors and shapes blend into a unifying presentation of the moment. The sky is blue and clear. In the linden treetops, cardinals are singing. Men walk by with their German shepherds on leashes; ladies carry poodles in their arms. A gray cat sits on the steps of the gazebo. The scent of juniper infuses my spirit with vigor. This is my truth. It is fragmented only in a sense that it unfolds in segments, scene after scene, snapshot after snapshot. Underneath, every move is imbedded in stillness.

Yes, this may not be the employment I dreamt of, but it is easy, and it pays $100 per hour. For a person who doesn't think money, $100 per hour crosses my mind too often. I took it not because I thought this particular line of work by itself suited me and would bring me fulfillment, but because this is life, and life is art, and art is fulfilling. If I were not already fulfilled would I have done it to fulfill my personal needs? No! But I found great satisfaction in knowing that this is my contribution to the fulfillment of Martin's dream.

TWENTY-SIX

"Hi Martin, I'm on my way," I said on the phone. "Meet you at the curve."

"If I make it," he paused, "in this traffic."

I could hear in his voice and the way he spoke with a slight resistance that he was disappointed more than normal, and I drove fast.

I dropped off the van in front of Namaste's house and ran. It was only a four-block run, but the fear that I might not be able to meet him at the curve made me anxious, and I used the last speck of energy to push my body to make it to where the road bent.

As soon as I turned onto Hoover, I saw the red CRV almost turning into the apartment complex parking. Not watching my steps in a hurry, I slipped on an edge of the sidewalk and fell down. I stifled my 'ouch' and just sighed instead, and without losing a second, got up and as soon as Martin got out of the car, I embraced him and held him. He held me back.

We walked towards the apartment.

"I reduced it to two days a week," he said.

"Okay," I said softly.

"I just couldn't continue working with dull burs, and rusty hand-pieces."

"It's okay, we will be fine."

"Why are you saying that? You always say that, and it's never fine. What could be fine? Nothing is fine."

"There are no limitations but those we impose upon ourselves," I said.

"Do you hear yourself, Marie? You speak nonsense."

"Things can get better, they always do," I said.

"What are you talking about?"

"Remember, just a couple of years ago you were driving a used beat-up car. Now you are driving a new car."

"That is nothing, everyone can get a new car, no down payment and zero interest."

"Okay, but for a long time we were in different schools and saw each other two or three times a year. Now we are together."

"And how well are we doing? Educated people living in poverty."

"We are paying our bills, and we live comfortably."

"Except that I am almost jobless, and you are unable to find a job."

We got into the apartment. I washed my hands and checked my knee. It was scratched and bleeding a little. *This isn't going to look good in the gazebo.* I cleaned the wound, applied Neosporin, and put on a Band-Aid. I washed my hands again before making a sandwich for Martin.

"The most important thing is that we have each other," I said from the kitchen.

"You are destroying my self-confidence, Marie," Martin

slammed the magazine to the floor. "I feel like a failure. I failed as a professional, I failed as a husband, and you have destroyed me with your nonsense."

My body shook for a moment, but I continued making Martin's sandwich.

"How can you be so calm? What is wrong with you?" Martin yelled, panthering around the living room.

"It isn't that I am not concerned, it's just that I am not expressing it because it doesn't help," I said.

"How can you not express it? You just don't give a damn, do you?" He sat on the couch and turned on the TV.

"Of course I do," I placed Martin's tray on the couch.

Martin looked at the food.

"Why did you put so much lettuce?" He glared at me. "How many times did I tell you I like small portions?"

I quickly grabbed a handful of lettuce from the plate and shoved it into my mouth.

"This marriage cannot be sustained. We are so different," he shook his head.

"We as people are all different, and we always need to adjust to each other," I said. "But deep inside we are all the same."

"You are driving me crazy with your philosophy. It would be better if you actually did something useful. You are distracting me. Look, it is getting late and I have not finished a single article," he shook his head in disgust, and grabbed a magazine from the floor.

I took a shower and went to the bedroom, opened my laptop and logged into my bank account. The balance was almost thirty thousand.

"Yes!" I slapped the bed triumphantly.

TWENTY-SEVEN

It was a slow morning. As the sun moved to the top of the sky, a few people walked along the sidewalk outside the four-foot fence. The sweet scent of rambling roses wrapped around the columns of the gazebo infused the air and made me a little drowsy. Depending on the breeze, some days I could sense the juniper fragrance coming from bushes surrounding the house, which always felt so refreshing. But today, the breeze was coming from the opposite direction.

"I cannot save Martin," my lips whispered suddenly.

My mind alerted to this shock I tried to process. Quickly I realized that this thought came on its own with a complete sense of self-sufficiency, and that I did not need to investigate it any further. My body relaxed to the point of lifelessness, and I slouched a little as I stood with my arms stretched to the sides of the gazebo.

I am not a God, I reasoned.

The faint sound of a tambourine came my way from far away, and I was sure it was more a part of my inner experience than a part of the external environment.

But the sound grew fuller. Guitar and drums accompanied

the tambourine, and singing could be more and more discerned behind the rumbling of a rusty engine. Soon, an old ruin of a school bus pulled up by the gate. I watched the back and side doors open simultaneously, and a bunch of people jumped out and sang and danced approaching the fence.

As they cavorted on the sidewalk in front of me, just 50 feet away, I could discern the words of their signature chant. "Hare Krishna, Hare Rama, Hare Krishna, Hare Hare," they sang and danced waving their arms in the air. "You are Krishna, you are Rama, you are Vishva, Hare Hare…"

A cloud of smoke gathered above the group, and I couldn't tell if they raised a bit of dust with their dancing, or if the smoke from the old engine caught in the tree branches and lingered there. A smell of patchouli mixed with the smell of sweat, dust, and exhaust from the bus reached me quickly.

The group lifted one member on their shoulders, and he spoke to the spectators gathering by the gate. "The Universe is speaking to you through this woman. Our human body is made of stardust. It is cosmic. To admire the body is to admire the creator. This woman is a voice of the Universe. We are the Universe, Hare Hare."

I saw George walk towards the group.

"No smoking, please. No weed," he kept saying, making sure everyone in the group could hear him, then went back towards the gate and stood there collecting fees from those who wished to come inside the fence closer to the gazebo.

A commotion arose within the singing group. They checked their pockets and produced some paper money but mostly coins, which they accidentally dropped on the sidewalk. I could hear coins jingling against concrete, and I could see Hare Krishnas get down on all fours to look for change scattered between the legs of startled people waiting in line to get inside the yard.

No one expected they would be able to collect enough money to get in, nor that they would want to spend whatever money they had on this event. Yet without much delay, the entire group lined up at the gate. George counted money and let them in one by one.

In the yard, they hurried towards me singing louder and dancing faster. As they faced me, they stood right in front of three ladies sitting on lawn chairs eating burritos.

"Really?!" One of the ladies exclaimed while chewing.

Without paying attention to the ladies behind them, the group looked at me with curiosity and reverence, as if I were some rare species, perhaps just landed from another planet.

"They are blocking our view," another of the three ladies said and looked around for George.

"The body is our temple, it is sacred," a tattooed red-headed girl from the group declared.

"That's why you should take a shower," one of the three ladies barked from behind.

"Quiet, Cynthia," another lady whispered loudly.

"I know you think this is art, Samantha, but this looks to me like honey," Cynthia said.

"I told Jim everything about it while we had our coffee this morning, and he didn't seem to think anything of it," Valerie said. "But, boy, the coffee was delicious, I got a French press and I added some cinnamon, and it tasted like…"

"What do you mean, it is 'honey'? What is wrong with you ladies? It is the bikini woman," Samantha interrupted.

"Honey attracts bees, don't you know that?" Cynthia said.

"Jim and I love honey. According to the *Arabic Book of Coffee*, it is not wrong to put honey in your coffee. Some say it is good for your gall bladder," Valerie talked as she nibbled her bean burrito.

"I see no bees around here..." Samantha looked around.

"But you see men swarming like bees around her," Cynthia pointed.

Clicking her castanet, the redhead turned around and blasted at the three ladies, "And women!"

"Jesus Christ!" Cynthia crossed herself with her free hand.

"Once when I was visiting cousin Karl in Lower River Village down by Flatsuff, I was bitten by a bunch of bees," Valerie said. "Who in his clear mind would like to be stung by a bunch of wild bees? But my cousin Karl, God bless his soul, opened the bee hives and let them bite me...."

"It is good for you, you will never get arthritis," The redhead turned around and looked at Valerie, then joined the group playing castanet and singing.

"You are a bunch of pot-heads, pretending to live peace and love," Cynthia said.

"No, Cynthia!" Samantha touched Cynthia's arm, "Love and peace."

"Say something nice, dear," Valerie said.

"The truth is that we can see only who we are," the redhead said. "Take this," she dropped a jingler in Cynthia's lap.

"Ahhh!" Cynthia screamed.

"It isn't a snake, it's a chime," the redhead said. "Do it like this," she held the handle of the chimes and demonstrated.

Cynthia watched, shaking her head.

"See?" the redhead put the instrument back into Cynthia's lap.

"I am not a musician. I am a secretary." Cynthia picked up the instrument with two fingers.

"Hold it like this, dear," the redhead adjusted Cynthia's fingers and then moved her hand rhythmically.

Reluctantly Cynthia continued, and quickly got into the rhythm.

Valerie and Samantha watched Cynthia's training session and performance with their mouths open, the burritos in their hands forgotten.

"Cynth, you are a good jingler," Valerie said.

"You are a natural," Samantha added.

Once Cynthia got into the rhythm, she started swaying and dancing in her chair. "It is addictive," she said.

The redhead glanced at her, grabbed her arm and pulled her up. "Come," she said.

Samantha and Valerie watched Cynthia mingle with the group, swaying her plump hips as the group moved.

Samantha looked at her watch. "Jesus! We need to get back to the office."

"We cannot go back without Cynthia," Valerie said.

"Cynthia!" Samantha called.

"She can't hear you," Valerie said. "We need to go get her now! Our lunch break was over twelve minutes ago and it will take at least six minutes to get there." They dumped their paper napkins and empty coffee cups in a trash can.

"Let's join the *corps de ballet*, shall we?" Samantha scoffed, dragging Valerie behind her. "Excuse me, sorry, let us get through, please," Samantha kept saying.

"Dance, dance…" the group recited, and spontaneously, almost without their will, the two ladies started moving their bodies with the swaying of the group.

No one can save anyone. God alone is our savior, I thought watching the crowd.

I cannot save Martin, I accepted. *But that doesn't mean I shouldn't try*, I smiled to myself.

TWENTY-EIGHT

A week after his first visit, Officer Ready marched into the scene. He took more photographs of Marie in the gazebo.

"Why are you here?" he approached a well-dressed middle-aged man.

"Hello, Officer. I like to look at this woman. Her body is completely open. She's a magnet, don't you agree?"

"Is this art, or does she get you excited?"

"Frankly, a little bit of both!" answered the man.

"I thought so," said the big policeman, writing on his pad.

"Now, young fellow, why are you here?" The officer confronted a young man with a backpack deeply focused on Marie in the gazebo.

"I should be somewhere else. I know I will regret this. As we speak, my advanced calculus class at the University is happening, but I can't help myself. This is better than the Internet! See, you can watch her breathe, in and out. Her body expands when she breathes in and contracts when she breathes out." He looked at the policeman's badge. "It's very subtle, Officer 558. Can you see what I see?" The young man shifted his glasses on the bridge of his nose.

"Not exactly. I'm looking at her legs and abdomen and chest and her face. There's too much exposure. It's indecent, don't you think, young fellow?"

"You may be right, Officer. But I could handle even more exposure. In my mind, she's way too covered up in that bikini. I want to watch her breathe all over! This is living art at its best!"

"Young man, leave the premises before it's too late. Go to your Cactus class!"

"Calculus, Officer."

"Don't talk back. This is an order." Officer Ready pointed down the street. "Don't hang around here. It's dangerous."

Officer Ready stepped towards a tall, attractive, elderly lady. "Good morning, Ma'am," he said. "Why are you here?"

Almost as tall as the policeman, slender figure, perfect posture, she smiled mischievously, "Speaking to me, handsome?"

"Uh, yes. I sure was." Their eyes locked in. "Why are you here?"

"You're a good-looking man," she checked him out.

"You're not bad yourself, Ma'am."

"I used to be a fashion model, you know, in our big cities, and occasionally in France and Italy. Every once in a while, even now, there's a job."

His blood warmed to color his cheeks. "I believe you. Now, why are you here?"

"Honest answer?" she said.

"The whole truth, Ma'am, and nothing but the whole truth!"

She caressed his shoulder. "I want to be doing exactly

what she's doing right now." She licked her lips. "This is what art should do — make us long for more of life, more openness, more closeness with others around us!" She stepped closer to him. "If I had my bikini with me, I'd volunteer! Isn't she one of the most luxuriant women you ever saw? You should have seen *me* thirty years ago!" She whispered into his ear, "You would have begged me to take my clothes off!"

The policeman avoided her eyes misting over. "But is it appropriate behavior to be tied to those posts like that, almost naked, facing these people, every day, day in and day out? It's indecent, don't you agree?"

"When you put it like that, it may be indecent to tie her stretched out like that. But, my God, she's beautiful! I wish I were her!" the woman's voice trailed off.

Officer Ready watched the woman sway her hips as she strolled away, exhaled a whistle, then took out his citation pad. He started writing in longhand. "Indecent Exposure Offense. Deliberate exposure in view of the public by a woman of virtually the entirety of her body, in circumstances where the exposure is contrary to local moral or other standards of decent behavior, to wit, standing virtually naked, her arms stretched out, with her wrists bound to opposite posts in a gazebo. In full view of the public." He underlined "contrary to local moral or other standards of decent behavior." And he added in capital letters, "Offense proven by three witnesses about local standards of decency."

He knocked hard at the gallery front door. "Here is something for your continuing criminal display, Mister Harris!" he handed the citation to George.

"Thank you again, Officer," said George. "Seriously, now, Officer, do you want to hear my side of this artistic installation?"

"Not at all! See you Friday, at 9:00 a.m. in Courtroom 1." The officer turned around to make sure George could hear him. "Oww!" he grimaced, as he bumped his forehead against a planter.

TWENTY-NINE

Howard stood in the linden tree shade leaning against the "LIVE ART GALLERY" sign, observing Marie in the gazebo. Even more closely he observed the spectators waiting in file to enter the gate. Only a few people were standing outside the file, and Howard couldn't help but notice how absorbed they were in the exhibit.

"Nice, ah?" He said to the young man sitting on top of the wall supporting the "LIVE ART GALLERY" sign.

"Nice?" The young man said, glancing through his long bangs at Howard. "No!"

"No? Why 'no'?" Howard said.

"The word is like dirt, dude."

"What do you mean 'like dirt'?"

"What do I mean? You suck, that's what I mean," the young man shook his head without diverting his eyes from the exhibit.

"Why don't you tell me what you see?" Howard asked.

"Dude, I see everything. It's my job."

"Everything?"

"I see a humbleness of purity that feeds upon flesh

imbued in the fleshless beauty of ether, of air, of nothing," the young man said.

"Tell me more," Howard said softly, looking at Marie with wide opened eyes.

"Why waste words? You got two eyes!"

"Tell me, what would you say to a blind man?"

"I would say, you are lucky you cannot see with your eyes, because a genuine piece of art is not seen on the level of sight."

"Is not?" Howard looked at the display.

"Can you see the totality?" the young man asked.

"I don't know, I never saw the totality. What does it look like?"

"It is within the boundaries of lines and shapes, but could not be contained by line nor color nor shape."

"Aha. And?"

"And just is. Like something that cannot be anything else but what it is to that absolute degree at which it actually could merge with lots of things, perhaps with everything, and therefore become a reflection of everything."

"But in this case...."

"In what case? There is no case, dude, no case!" the young man insisted.

"I mean, in this live art presentation ... What do you see in it?" Howard asked.

"I see the light," the young man said.

"And how does it look?"

"It looks like a birch tree, like a seagull. White and light and graceful. It has La Gioconda's calmness, Venus' innocence, and the grace of Jesus...." Struggling to find words while staring at Marie under thin strands of hair, the man got quiet.

"Young man, you are painting a picture that in my mind looks vivid and extraordinary, a picture I would pay a fortune to have on my wall," Howard broke the silence.

"You have Mona Lisa on live display, and you would rather have a painting on your wall? Dude, that's sick!"

"All I am saying is that if what you see can be put on canvas, I would want to have it."

"It is too late," the young man said.

"Too late?"

"Sorry to break the news to you, but Da Vinci and Botticelli and Rubens are dead," the young man said.

"Could you perhaps put on paper what you described to me?"

"What are you talking about?"

"Can you write it down?"

"No. I am no writer," said the young man.

"What are you, if I may ask?"

"I am an artist, dude, a painter, isn't that obvious?"

"If you were up to it, I would like to commission the painting of what you see and would pay good money," Howard said.

"I don't know that I can do her justice."

THIRTY

Friday morning, the accused defendant George Harris and his lawyer Frank Master walked into Courtroom One. "Frank, this installation is art, plus, for that matter, with the questionnaire, it's science. There's nothing indecent about Marie in my gazebo!"

"I understand, George. Let me do the talking, okay?"

"Sure, Frank. You know what to say."

"No kidding, George!"

The prosecutor, Doc Ashton, spotted Master immediately. "Frank! Frank, you and your guilty client come over here. I need to talk to you!"

"If you want to dismiss this charge like you did the obscenity charge, that's fine with me, Doc." Frank Master smiled.

"Well, Frank, no, I can't do that. See, I interpret the indecent exposure law more broadly than the obscenity charge. Anyway, obscenity usually refers to books and films. But so-called live art, now that can get *indecent* in a hurry! And the officer has witnesses."

"Witnesses to what, Doc? Everybody knows what's going on. We have photographs. She's wearing a bikini."

"Ha! The officer has witnesses to standards of morality and society's standards of decency, that's what! We can proceed with this charge of indecent exposure. Officer Ready is going to testify what his witnesses stated. Plus, we have a new courtroom and a new judge!"

"Doc!" cautioned Frank Master. "There's no exposure, you know; no exposure of her genitals or nipples, no matter how many witnesses or new judges you've got!"

A bailiff's voice boomed across the room, "All rise, the Honorable Rush Robinson, District Court Judge, is now presiding. Silence is commanded! Be seated!"

The prosecutor moved forward, followed by Frank Master and George Harris. Officer Ready and the prosecutor took seats at one table and the defendant and his lawyer took seats at another.

The clerk announced, "People versus Harris, Indecent Exposure."

"Mr. Ashton, are you prosecuting?" The judge inquired.

"Yes, Your Honor," Doc answered.

"This is a preliminary hearing to determine if there is enough evidence to proceed to trial at a later date," the judge announced. "Call your witness, Mr. Ashton."

"Your Honor," Frank Master jumped up. "There's no exposure of genitals or nipples in this case," his big courtroom voice echoed. "Here are the prosecution's own photographs!" He held up the photos. "She's wearing a bikini at all times! Judge ...."

"Thank you, Mr. Master," Judge Robinson interrupted, "You'll get your chance. Let's hear what the officer has to say. By the way, Doc, is that true about no exposure of genitals or nipples?"

"Yes, Your Honor, but this case is constructed on public standards of morality, social standards of decency, like the law prohibits."

"'Constructed' is right, Judge," added Frank Master.

The judge gave defense counsel a stern look. "Call your witness, Mr. Ashton!"

"Officer Everett Ready!"

The big policeman sat in the witness stand facing the spectators. The benches were packed.

"State your name, please," said the prosecutor.

The witness tapped the microphone once, then said, "Officer Everett Ready, Badge Number Five Five Eight, police officer."

"Officer, please read your citation of the charge in this case, and then tell us your underlying evidence to support the charge, if you would, please," Ashton said.

"Yes, sir. The citation I prepared and delivered to the defendant, Mr. Harris, over there," the officer pointed his fleshy finger at the defendant, "reads as follows: 'Indecent Exposure Offense. Deliberate exposure in view of the public by a woman of virtually the entirety of her body, in circumstances where the exposure is contrary to local moral or other standards of decent behavior, to wit, standing virtually naked, her arms stretched out, with her wrists bound to opposite posts in a gazebo. In full view of the public. Offense proven by three witnesses about local standards of decency.'"

The policeman continued, "That's the citation, Your Honor. Now, the circumstances are that the defendant's employee, the woman, is standing in the center of a raised gazebo, naked except for the slightest bikini, with her arms outstretched to the side posts of the gazebo, where her wrists are bound to the posts, fully facing the onlookers, maybe twenty-five to thirty feet away, on the public sidewalk. There's a crowd gathered there looking, leering at her lewd body, her arms stretched in a bondage situation."

"Did you make photographs of this indecent display, Officer," the prosecutor interjected, "and if so, please hand copies to the Court."

"These are photographs I took that day, just as she was, Your Honor." He handed them to the clerk, who handed them to the judge.

"Your Honor," added the prosecutor, "I have already provided copies of these photographs to defense counsel."

"Do you have copies, Mr. Master?" the judge asked.

"I do, Your Honor."

"Have you looked at them?"

"Many times, Your Honor!"

"Please continue with your evidence, Mr. Ashton," directed the judge.

"Thank you, Your Honor." Ashton turned to the witness. "Officer Ready, did you have occasion to interview several witnesses at this lewd display, to memorialize a sense of society's standards of decency or standards of morality regarding this indecent display?"

"I did."

"And what did those witnesses state to you?"

"I interviewed a well-dressed middle-aged male, who stated, 'I like to look at this woman. Her body is completely open.' I asked him, 'Does she get you excited?' he answered 'Yes.' I interviewed a male college student, who admitted, 'I should be at the university. I can't help myself. This is better than the Internet!' Your Honor, we know what's on the

Internet! This student added, 'You can watch her breathe, in and out.' Next, I interviewed an attractive, older lady who stated, 'It's indecent to tie her stretched out like that.' That's my summary of evidence, Your Honor."

"Any questions, Mr. Master?" asked the judge.

"Yes, Your Honor." Frank Master stood in front of the witness. "Officer Ready, do you feel it is your duty to protect people who need to be protected?"

"Yes, that is my duty."

"And, Officer, is it also your duty to protect people who do not know they need to be protected?"

"Yes, of course, that is my duty."

"And I take it, Officer Ready, it is your duty to protect people who want to be protected, isn't that true?"

"Certainly I protect people who want to be protected."

"Isn't it true that from time to time you are called upon to protect people who do not want to be protected?"

"I do not hesitate to protect them."

"Objection, Your Honor," chimed Doc Ashton. "Irrelevant."

"Where is this going, Mr. Master? Get to the point!"

"One final question, Judge." Master looked at the witness. "Now, Officer, isn't it also true that your sworn duty is to protect people who neither want nor need to be protected, when you get right down to it?"

"I protect them, no matter what."

"No further questions, Your Honor."

"Thank you, Officer Ready. You may step down," the judge said. "Would the prosecution want to take this opportunity to apply its evidence to the law?"

"Yes, Your Honor," said the prosecutor, firing a challenging stare at Frank Master. "Indecent Exposure is a fluid law, grounded in social morality and public standards of decency. What falls outside these standards is indecent exposure. As we have just heard, the defendant's employee, a woman, standing stretched bound to opposite posts of a raised gazebo, no doubt very much surprised and shocked passers-by who gathered to leer at her lewd display, clearly intended to arouse. This is more than virtual nudity in a public place. There is a definite indecent element in this display! As the middle-aged man stated, 'I get excited.' As the college student stated, 'I can't help myself. This is better than the Internet.' It is precisely this indecent element which makes such public behavior indecent. Society's standards in this regard are voiced by the older lady's clear statement to the officer, 'It's indecent to tie her stretched out like that.' It is precisely this indecent exposure which must be prosecuted, Your Honor."

"Thank you, Mr. Ashton," said the judge. "As always, you and your witness have given us much to think about."

The judge turned his gaze to the defense lawyer. "I want very much to hear from Mr. Frank Master, on behalf of his client, the defendant George Harris. However, if Mr. Master will indulge me, before I call on him, it is incumbent upon me to make a few remarks."

The judge held the photographs above his head for all to see. "Here are the photographs of a barely clothed woman, a beautiful woman in a minimal bikini. She is not naked. I note at the onset that even depictions of complete nudity have often been considered art, from literature to paintings to movies. The defendant's employee in this case is not even naked; there is no nudity here. These are the prosecution's own photographs."

The defendant started to stand up, but his attorney Frank Master pulled him down hard, back into his chair. "Sit still, George! Be quiet and sit still!" he whispered.

The judge continued, "Nevertheless, there may be an issue for a jury if the exposure offends against public decency. The phrase indecent exposure requires something more active, with greater moral turpitude, than a mere state of exposure, whether or not the subject may be bound to posts of a gazebo."

The judge looked around his crowded courtroom. "With regard to the crime of indecent exposure, the 'greater moral turpitude' I just referred to is uniformly demonstrated by proof of genital exposure or a woman's nipples." The crowd shifted quietly in their seats. "This display must occur in a public place," the judge continued, "such as we have in this case. ... While society's standards may change from time to time, Officer Ready, the *sine qua non* of indecent exposure does not change; it is public exposure of genitalia or a woman's nipples."

When the judge said his name, the big policeman bolted as if to stand up, but the prosecutor pulled him down hard, back into his chair. "Sit still, Ever! Be quiet and sit still!" he ordered.

Judge Robinson looked around. He saw the entire courtroom on edge — spectators, lawyers, defendants, policemen and deputies looking up at him, waiting for his next words. He paused in that moment of stillness.

The defendant George Harris fidgeted. Frank Master sat completely relaxed, his lips hiding a subtle smile.

"At this preliminary stage," said the judge, "our inquiry is whether or not the prosecution has sufficiently stated a *prima facie* case of probable guilt of the crime charged, that is, does the evidence presented by the officer tend to show the offense of indecent exposure or not? My duty is to make that decision."

Judge Robinson nodded at Officer Ready. "The officer's testimony is clear. He has presented a provocative display of living art. Photographs submitted by the officer show a beautiful woman wearing a bikini. It is clear he has presented no evidence whatsoever of exposed genitalia or nipples. I refer counsel to the celebrated *Hilton* case! The officer has presented no conduct on her part that would be likely to prove indecency. It is not unheard of for a woman to be dressed in a bikini. By now, we are all used to that. A thousand witnesses cannot convert these facts into indecent exposure!"

"Sure," murmured some spectators. "That's right," the crowd nodded agreement.

"I say to you," continued the judge, "the prosecution has failed to present even *prima facie* proof of the offense charged, indecent exposure."

Judge Robinson looked directly at Frank Master. "In light of my comments, does defense counsel wish to make a motion at this time?"

Frank Master's smile emerged from its hiding place, as he stood to address the Court. "Your Honor has spoken the very words I had prepared to say. Nothing is clearer. On behalf of the defendant George Harris, the defense moves the Court to enter an Order dismissing the charge of indecent exposure, with prejudice."

"'With prejudice,' counsel?" the judge looked at Master.

"With prejudice, Your Honor! This is not the first time

this policeman has charged this defendant."

"Another charge, counsel?" the judge asked Master.

"Yes, Your Honor. Previously, this same officer, Officer Ready, over there," the lawyer pointed his manicured finger at the policeman, "issued another citation charging Obscenity, based on identical facts as we heard today, which the prosecutor wisely declined to prosecute, and obtained dismissal in Courtroom Two with my agreement. Now, our point is that it would be a great injustice to have this defendant subjected to additional citations issued by this officer in the days and weeks to come, based on these same facts, as I regret to predict he may attempt to impose."

"Very well, Mr. Master, the Court grants your motion to dismiss," the judge ruled. "Furthermore, the Court orders dismissal with prejudice, meaning the prosecution is barred from bringing any other related charges in the future against this defendant."

A murmur arose again in the courtroom. A woman's voice called out, "Frank Master wins again!"

Judge Robinson ignored the outburst. He continued, "I feel compelled to remark in supplementation of my ruling of dismissal, that erotic art, even living art, is protected by the First Amendment. What may appeal to a policeman's prurient interest may be run-of-the-mill and commonplace live art for others in society. When associated with an art gallery, examples of provocative art are expected. What distinguishes one art gallery above another, in capturing the public's interest, is the greatness of free speech. It is creativity in competition. This display of a woman standing on the raised floor of a gazebo, with arms stretched out, in my opinion, presents convincing artistic and social value for our community."

"Thank you, Your Honor," said Frank Master.

George Harris stood beside his lawyer. "I thank you, Judge. Thank you so much!" He snapped his suspenders.

"What have you done to me, Ever?" Doc Ashton scolded Officer Ready.

"Doc, these bikini women are evil. They will excite you and hurt you!"

"Everett, now what are you talking about?"

"It's a long story, Doc!"

"I want to hear it, but not right now. You seem to be projecting some personal issue. And, by the way, what is that Band-Aid on your forehead?"

"Self-defense, Doc!"

Judge Robinson hit the bench with his gavel, "Madam Clerk, call the next case!"

THIRTY-ONE

Standing in the gazebo sometimes I possessed extrasensory perception. I was so quiet and still within myself, I could hear people talking to each other far away, as if I were there.

"See, Howard, all these people." I watched George scan the full range of his yard from the street to the fence behind the gazebo, then recline in his lawn chair and sip his Piña Colada. "They are coming every day to see our live art display because it is unique. Also, not to sound too smug, the management is superb. It would not surprise me if this is one of your best investments ever, and considering everything, if you offered me a raise, which you should, I would accept."

"I see, George, things are going smooth. That's all I want to hear," Howard finished his drink and got up. "I'll keep the money coming." He buttoned his Armani jacket and took a few steps towards the gate.

"Thank you Howard. Without your financial support, this would never have happened. What would Michelangelo have done without Cosimo?" George walked behind Howard.

"Without who?" Howard stopped and turned around and looked at the gazebo. The crowd solemnly flowed, stopping in front of me, looking, then continuing towards the exit.

"DeMedici! Cosimo DeMedici," George explained.

"Right!" Howard extended his hand for a shake, "I'll stop by again, George, and you keep doing what you are doing. I see everything is under control here." They shook hands, congratulated each other, and gave each other a good clap on the shoulder.

Just as Howard started walking towards his car, a little commotion occurred within the crowd and a perfect tenor voice emerged.

"Oh, yes, I am wise
But it's wisdom born of pain
Yes, I've paid the price
But look how much I've gained
If I have to, I can do anything…"

Howard stopped and listened, "What is this, George?"

"It happens all the time, Howard. A spontaneous outburst of singing or dancing. People reflecting the joy of true art."

"Yes, yes, George. Great joy, indeed," Howard mumbled as he walked to his car, with the song still going on.

"I am strong
I am invincible
I am woman."

Three young men standing behind the tenor swayed their bodies in unison as they echoed "I am strong," "I am invincible," "I am woman" in high pitched tones.

The crowd's attention turned away from me towards the singer.

"That's 'I Am Woman,'" a plump lady said excitedly.

"What a voice!" another exclaimed.

"Why is he scowling?" A male voice asked.

As soon as Howard's car disappeared in the distance, George rushed towards the singers, "Welcome friends," he said, smiling broadly. "Come closer to view my live art presentation! I am George Harris, owner of the Live Art Gallery. And you, my friend?"

"I am Donald Lord, pastor of the Everland True Church of America. My friends and I have come to open your eyes to the truth," the man said in an exaggerated manner.

"Reverend Lord, you certainly have a fine lilting voice!"

"That is the voice of God," the pastor frowned, closed his eyes and raised his arms high above his head. Spectators watched with their mouths open as he slowly brought his arms down, his fists joined together. "Your lascivious display exudes shame and sin," he pointed at me. "This naked woman is a snare for innocent youth, and weak men and women! This naked woman causes everyone who beholds her to sink into the mire of their subconscious swamp until they drown in addictions of the flesh. Adam and Eve were not ashamed as long as they knew not they were naked. When they knew they were naked, they were ashamed of their nakedness, and they feared God. That is why they clothed themselves."

"Yes! With fig leaves!" someone yelled from the audience.

Pastor Donald turned to George, "Clothe this woman, gallery owner, so that the shame of her nakedness will not be revealed! Selah!"

"You speak like an artist, Pastor Donald, just as beautifully as you sing. Please continue," George said.

"Yea, the owner of the gallery speaks softly, although he is the shame of his community," Pastor Donald spoke to the visitors.

"Is this supposed to be for real, or is it staged?" a young man asked the pastor. A few viewers voiced the same concern.

"This is from *Shakespeare In Love*," a young girl said, "You know, with Gwyneth Paltrow."

"Mommy, Mommy, he's extemporating!" a chubby child pulled on his mother's jacket.

"Extemporizing, honey," the child's mother laughed, patting his head.

The pastor took a moment, looking into the distance, immersed in his own thoughts.

Suddenly everyone was shaken by the thunder of his voice, "In the name of the Lord!" The chubby boy grabbed his mother's skirt. "We should demand the gallery owner shut down this lewd display and stop this degradation of a woman in the name of art," the pastor concluded.

"I pay her, your, your…" George stuttered, struggling to find a proper word to address the pastor. "Your pastorship," he added.

The viewers were now certain this was a staged performance and, immersed, shifted their gaze from George to the pastor. "How much?" the pastor asked, and the viewers looked at George, curious to hear the answer.

"$100 per hour, Your Majesty," George blurted out.

Now all the eyes were on the pastor, who hesitated, as if considering that one hundred dollars an hour might not be degrading.

"Not bad, eh?" a voice came from the audience.

"I wish they paid me that much at Walmart," an older woman said.

For a while there was a commotion in the group, everyone agreeing with the voice from the back, approving of the amount, "Great pay, man," they said, and light applause scattered around the yard.

"This woman, her nakedness and shame therefore have lured these weak people into a snare of pure evil, into the many mindless and senseless and harmful desires that plunge people into ruin of destruction!" roared Donald the Pastor. "In the word of God, 'I say unto you that everyone who looks at a woman with lustful intent has already committed adultery with her in their hearts!' By exhibiting this naked woman, the owner somersaults us into separation from God, God the Almighty!" He raised his long index finger to the sky.

The crowd seemed confused.

A few men and women scowled at the preacher as they turned and walked away. "We're leaving!" they announced.

A college student said, "What is this guy?"

A tattooed topless truck driver grinned, "What's your problem, preacher? Leave the folks alone."

"These people are not lustful, my friend, they appreciate beauty which art radiates," George interjected, louder than before. "This live art expands their awareness, opens their minds and hearts to wider realms of existence, leading them to God. As you say, 'God the Almighty!'"

The remaining spectators who heard George's words muttered agreement.

"It's art to me, I like it."

"Isn't she beautiful?"

"I look at her and feel bigger and happier."

"Exciting!"

"That's right!"

The minister listened carefully to George's words and the onlookers' agreement. He nodded and mumbled under his breath, "one hundred dollars an hour, ha." An internal struggle took place for a moment, and it seemed he was speechless. Just when everyone thought he might have given up, his voice thundered, "Who is this charming one who shakes and destroys the foundations of society?"

"She is Marie, my employee," George interjected quickly, with pride in his full voice, so everyone could hear. "This is my art gallery and she is my live art installation. I am at your service, Pastor Lord. What exactly do you want?"

The minister stepped forward into George's face. Their eyes met. "We have come to close you down!" he declared.

After a noticeable pause, and since no one said anything, he continued. "If we allow you to continue your prurient pornographic display of shame and nakedness, blossoming in the soil of human weakness, undermining blessed gifts endowed to all by a loving God, God the Almighty will destroy you, your Marie, these people and others to come. We must close you down! Glory!" He finished, casting his arms heavenward!

George moved towards the pastor and whispered into his ear, "Do you want to speak with Marie?"

Donald Lord stopped cold. "That may be helpful," he blurted.

George led the minister off to the side for privacy. "You are a wonderful orator," he said, "An artist, like me! Do you want to speak with Marie?" he asked again.

The minister looked at the woman in the gazebo with her arms spread wide open. Against his will, he said, "Yes, of course, naturally."

He remembered the song. He recited the words in cadence. "I am woman, watch me grow, see me standing toe-to-toe, as I spread my loving arms across the land." He spread his wings wide open as he stared at me. "Her loving arms extending an invitation," he mumbled.

George's soothing voice resurfaced, "Let me confess, my friend, that the police tried twice to shut down this live art installation. Twice, the court considered the charges, first obscenity, and then indecent exposure. Twice, the court ruled we are not in violation of any law or legal standard of morality. The judge's Order even states categorically we are protected by the First Amendment. Just like you, my friend, are protected by the First Amendment when you march in here singing songs and preaching to onlookers peaceably observing live art!"

"Amendments are for sinners! *We* are not protected by amendments! We are protected by *Commandments*!" The minister turned to George. "We are protected by God Almighty! We are charged with the duty to march in here, singing and exhorting God's people, every day, day after day, until this sinful display is dismantled! I will make your spectators ashamed! I will drive them away!"

"You are welcome to try, friend. A-l-w-a-y-s welcome,"

George calmly answered. "I'll even contact the media to publicize your performances, so that your songs and words may be enjoyed on the evening news. I'll make my own videos of you and your friends and put them on the Internet. *You* will become a star. *Your* congregation will grow and prosper!"

"And yours will crumble like the walls of Jericho!" His hand slashed downward.

THIRTY-TWO

For weeks thereafter, the minister Donald Lord came singing with his chorus that grew from three to many. They came singing and exhorting, "Turn away from the woman's nakedness and thereby end your own sin, and stop her sin in its tracks!" He vowed, "My flock will disrupt this evil display for half an hour each day. We will drive away all of you!"

The press picked up the story. "God's Flock Decries Live Art," proclaimed a headline on the front page, with a picture of Marie in the gazebo. The *Andover Daily News* circulation increased. Television news covered the harsh minister's opposition to the beautiful woman. Don Lord's tenor voice rang out on TV.

He sang triumphantly.

"We are the champions, my friends,
And we'll keep on fighting 'til the end.
We are the champions.
We are the champions.
No time for losers
'Cause we are the champions of our Lord!"

Television news played his singing, while showing Marie in the gazebo. Wider and wider audiences tuned in.

Pastor Lord's oratory issued forth on the evening news. "Blessed is the one who stays awake and keeps her clothes. So that she will not walk about naked and men will not see her shame!"

The TV announcer praised "Pastor Lord's marvelous voice," while the camera framed Marie. "Minister Don Lord serves his God. He protects the weak from the temptations of the flesh." The camera zoomed in on Marie breathing, with her arms stretched out on both sides. "More and more men are joining the minister's flock every day," the announcer said,

"How did you decide to join Pastor Lord's church?" a reporter asked.

"I like art, but this is too much!" one recruit said.

"I had to see for myself this sinful display!" said another.

"I would have been embarrassed to come on my own," another said.

"How happy I am to be with the flock!" another added, "I always wanted to see the woman and with Pastor Lord, I feel protected from sin."

Media coverage increased Live Art Gallery attendance. George and Howard stood by the gazebo watching the crowd. "I've never been so famous," said George, "I'm being compared to Alexa Meade! People are turning more and more to live art!"

"Let them compare you to Picasso, I'm satisfied," Howard agreed. "Every day, more and more people appreciate our live art! Research is going to be a success."

Pastor Lord's congregation grew. "They worship God in

my singing," he said. "They serve God as my sermons direct. My church sings and shouts for the glory of God, God the Almighty! Selah!" He praised the men of his chorus, "My flock serves God and destroys this abomination of shameful sin, this snare for the weak and innocent! They see it for themselves!"

Newspaper, television and Internet editors were demanding, "I don't care if you've reported it thirty times. Get out there and find a new angle. This is front-page news! This is our lead story! Make more photos and videos of the woman! People appreciate art! It's about art! And cover the singing minister and his flock!"

Day in and day out, the minister was there. "This woman's nakedness and shame! What a snare that gives birth to senseless and shameful desires that plunge people into ruin and destruction! She separates them from God, God the Almighty!"

"A secret, friend," George confided later to Pastor Donald. "She admires you and thinks you're good-looking and cool. It's not about your message. She likes you as a man. It's strange how you've been here so many, many times, and the two of you never spoke a word."

The minister smoothed his hair with both palms but said nothing.

A few weeks later, Pastor Donald approached George, "We need to talk."

"Okay, Don. Let me get some tea for us." They sat together in lawn chairs, sipping chamomile tea. "Art is long, and live art wears well!" George said, "What you do is art, the singing and the sermons. You're all over TV and the Internet! See? I've made you famous!"

George lifted his arms like Moses.

"George, you know I know what you want," Donald frowned. "You want to ascend to the top of the innovative live art world. You want me to go away and let all these passersby and onlookers make their own wrong decisions about your presentation, don't you?" The minister swallowed some tea. "I have news for you, George. First, coffee suits me better than bland tea. And second, all this publicity about me singing, a man singing the anthem 'I Am Woman,' has borne fruit like seeds cast onto fertile ground."

"Yes, your flock multiplied," said George.

"With the grace of God, indeed it did! But the news is even more."

"What is it, Don?"

"The recording people called me. They like the way my voice covers Helen Reddy's classic song. They want me in L.A. to start a singing career. And New York too."

"Wonderful!" George said.

"My foot is in the door, my friend! You know what? I'm going to give it a try, with God's help!" He took a sip of tea, spit it onto the grass and leaned towards George, "I'm getting out of Dodge!"

THIRTY-THREE

I waited for Martin on the street, still thinking about the fluctuations on my ovulation chart that looked like a bird's wings spread wide against unforgiving grids on graph paper. Above the traffic, I heard my mother's voice, "Learn pole dancing, and fast."

Martin pulled close to the curb and stopped. As soon as I opened the car door, he warned me, "Don't slam the door!"

I closed the door softly.

"You didn't close it!" Martin said.

I tried a little bit harder.

"Marie, you must be kidding!" he said.

"No, I am just trying to figure out how to close with a minimum slam."

"Try a smidgen harder."

I pulled the door harder.

"Jesus, Marie, you don't know how to close the door?" Martin reached for the door handle. "Move away," he said and closed the door. "This is a simple thing Marie. How come you don't know how to close the door without slamming?"

I said nothing.

"Marie, are you ignoring me?" he was shocked.

"No, just don't know how to answer your question."

"How about you try in English?"

"Maybe the door is too heavy," I said.

"Maybe your muscles are too weak. How many times did I tell you to exercise?"

"I do…" I almost said, "I'm doing pole dancing!"

But Martin interrupted, "Don't tell me you do Yoga. Yoga is stretching, not exercising."

We got out of the car and walked to our apartment.

Martin washed his hands and sat on the couch and turned on the TV.

I prepared the dinner tray, placed it on the couch next to Martin, and sat at the table to eat my dinner. I looked at Martin from behind. The shifting light from the TV and the sunset streaming sideways through the window in a single vibrant wave enveloped his head making his aura beam with light expanding rapidly. The door of my memory opened wide.

I had called his house from the bus station seven times, and no one answered. I walked by his house, looking at the windows. All the lights were off. I waited for a while longer, as long as I could, not long at all, and rang the bell. "I am looking for Martin," I said to his mother, a beautiful fleshy woman.

"He is not here," she leaned against the doorframe.

"Do you have any idea when he might be back?"

"No, I don't," she said, framed within the door like a full body portrait, her arms spread, palms pushing against the frame sides. I realized I had come to a dead-end. My legs felt stiff, unwilling to get me down the stairs.

"If you want, come in," she said, without moving.

"Okay," I said, and before she got a chance to finish the sentence, I snuck under her arm into the house. Inside, it felt like a sanctuary, cold and serene, with only a few lights on.

She led me to an empty living room, pointed at a chair, and left.

"Lemonade?" she asked, holding a tray. "Where did you go for your summer vacation?" she asked, as she sat in a chair next to me.

"I visited my friend in Miami, just came back, straight from the bus station." I stirred the lemonade with a straw.

"A male friend, I assume," she said coldly.

"No, Denise, my friend from childhood."

"Ah! I see." She nodded. "Whether it is Dennis or Denise, I do not know. But we would like you to stay away from Martin."

"Why?" I barely said, when we heard the entrance door open.

"It is him," she announced and walked out of the living room. "Martin, you have a visitor," I heard her say.

I stood up, waiting to hear him ask, "Who is it?" but he didn't. He slowly walked into the half-lit living room, looking at the floor, his mother right behind him. As soon as he looked up, his face lit up the room with a smile. "You are back," he said as we embraced. "You are the best thing that happened to me today," he said, as we held onto each other.

As the reverie faded, I took my plate and sat on the floor by Martin's feet and continued eating. He dropped his magazine on the floor, took the tray from the couch, put it on his knees and, with his index finger, he pointed at the piece of garlic bread.

"Is this butter?"

"Yes," I stopped chewing my food.

"Why did you put butter on my bread?" he asked.

"It was part of the recipe I found online."

"You want me to get a heart attack and die? Is that what you want?" he demanded.

"Here, I will take it," I quickly grabbed the piece of garlic bread and flopped it on my plate, then got up and cut off a slice of bread, "You want a piece of plain bread?" I offered.

Martin grabbed it, folded it lengthwise, and bit on it. "Marie, you are not going to eat all that butter, are you?" he said.

"Yes, I am," I said.

"No, you are not!" he reached for my plate.

I quickly moved the plate away and, looking at Martin, shoved the entire chunk of garlic bread into my mouth.

"You will get a heart attack, Marie! Even worse, you will get fat, you already have a good layer of fat," he pinched the side of my body about waist level. "See?" he said.

"I am not going to waste food, butt…."

"Don't say the word!" Martin interrupted. "I hate the sound of it."

"It isn't as bad for you as they say."

"True, it is worse!"

Focused on switching channels with his right-hand pinky, he managed to affectionately nudge my shoulder with his elbow, and I pushed back gently.

I do not find TV news entertaining, so I watched absentmindedly.

"Wow! Mousy watching news!" Martin was surprised to see me still sitting there.

With all the coverage surrounding the Live Art Gallery and the gazebo, it's good Martin normally watches national rather than local news, I thought. I knelt in front of Martin and embraced him, my head resting on his shoulder.

He leaned his head against mine. "It is almost 10 p.m., Mousy, you need to go to sleep before they catch you," he teased.

"Good night. Love you," I said and got up from the floor to go to bed.

"Marie," I heard Martin's voice behind me.

"Yes?" I turned around.

"Why did you say that?" he asked.

"What?"

"Are you not aware of what you are saying?"

"I said good night and ..."

"And?"

"And I love you."

"So why are you always saying 'I love you'? What do you want to accomplish by saying it all the time?" he asked.

"I feel it and that's why I say it," I said.

"You think it is necessary to always say things you feel?"

"No, just when I feel I want to."

"You are wasting my time with useless emotionality that has no practical value," he said.

"Love has practical value," I said.

"How is your love practical? Of what use is your love to me now?"

"It should mean something..."

"Whatever it means, it is useless to me. I am here trying to save my career and my life, and you are talking feelings."

"I want to make you feel good."

"You don't need to make me feel good. I don't need to

feel good, I need to accomplish something in this life."

"You are doing your best," I said.

"You see? That's what is so disappointing about you," he said. "A *good wife* would have pushed her husband to achieve something. And you, you make me feel weak and useless with your emotional talk. Emotions! Who cares about emotions? You are killing me with your emotions."

"Okay, I won't say anything. It's okay...."

"For you, Marie, everything is okay. Just close your eyes and ignore the reality. Jesus, you are worse than I thought...."

I knelt in front of Martin again and looked at his face.

"Go to sleep, Marie. I am fighting for my life so that I can help you, so that I can take care of you and our children, if we get to the point to have any, and you are pushing me deeper and deeper into the abyss."

"Sorry, I don't mean to...."

"You are so naïve Marie, you are killing me with your naïveté. Go, go, leave me alone or I am going to explode. You are going to make me do stupid things."

"I cannot go to bed with your feelings hurt," I sobbed.

"Then do whatever you want. Move away! I need to watch TV, to be informed, Marie. I need to read."

I didn't move away, but took Martin's face in both my hands and looked closely into his eyes. I wanted to tell him that I was working, that I got some money for him, but instead I said, "Don't worry, everything is going to be fine. I can work. I can help." I kissed his forehead and his cheeks.

"Yes, $10 per hour is going to be very, very helpful," he said calmly, wiping my tears from his face.

"The most important thing is that we are together." I

hugged him, my head on his chest. Not knowing what else to say, I started softly singing a song my grandmother sang to me when I was a child.

"On a lovely summer day
Little daisies decided to play
With the breeze they sway
Forever best friends,
Through the air they sweep
Their dream swells
Into sleep, sleep, sleep
Sweeter than sweet."

I sniffled as I sang and rocked Martin gently. His breathing got quiet. Looking at the TV screen over my shoulder, he kept switching channels on the remote he held behind my back. I sang more and more quietly, and when I heard the late show theme music, I stopped, kissed Martin's cheek and went to the bedroom.

I opened my laptop and checked my bank account. *As if checking my bank account every night would somehow make the balance grow*, I laughed at myself. *The same as yesterday $99,400.* I went to bed and stared at the darkness until my eyes got tired. As they closed by themselves, I watched myself falling asleep while on TV, the Mercedes dealership commercial blasted the *Mercedes Girl Song* through our apartment. *"She's the wunderkind where the rainbow ends, at money, love, and Mercedes-Benz!"*

THIRTY-FOUR

At the DailyFix coffee shop, George teased Howard, "Cappuccino? You are cheating on Americano!"

"Cannot help it George, I love them both," Howard said, cradling his cup in his hands.

"Okay, my mouth is sealed." George zipped his lips.

"That's why I'm paying you," Howard laughed then touched the corners of his lips with a gold-monogrammed handkerchief. "So, we almost allowed people to speak to her, eh?"

"At first, we had people watch her from the sidewalk, about 50 feet from the gazebo. Then, at their request, we allowed them to get inside the yard, 20 feet from the gazebo, and even sit in front of her and take their time feeling what they are feeling while watching her so they can fill out the questionnaire properly, just what they wanted, and just what we need. Once they came closer to Marie, they wanted to talk to her. You go figure!"

"What did Marie think about that?"

"She said, 'George, you talk to them.'"

"She is smart!" Howard said.

George sipped his cappuccino. "I told them, 'talk to me,' but they laughed at me. They looked at me, top to bottom, 'You are kind of cute, but you are not live art, are you?' 'No,' I said, 'Marie is.' 'If she is live art, why can't we talk to her?' they said. I explained to them that this is not an entertainment thing. Then they said, 'Can we write notes to her?'"

"They can write whatever they want on the questionnaire!" Howard said.

"The spectators wanted personal contact," George bit a piece of chocolate almond biscotti. "I discussed it with Marie."

"What did she say?"

"She said, 'You see, George, the project has a life of its own.'"

"True! That's what I said at the beginning!" He studied the bikini girl poster. "The unexpected arises in any kind of business."

"The questionnaires keep pouring in," George said. "It's ongoing. I've got a stack a foot high. We do nothing and they tell us everything. What they feel when they look, what they want in life, failures and disappointments, hopes and beliefs, secret dreams — more than we want to know."

"But what does it all mean?"

"Professor Higgins in Sociology at the University has agreed to organize the responses and draw conclusions! We're going to shake up the art world, Howard!"

"We will solve the mystery!" said Howard. "Why men look at women!"

"As well as why women look at women."

"That too. We will get to the bottom of it all!"

"Yes, we will," George agreed.

"Good job! Go ahead, George. Let me know how much we need to pay this professor of yours."

"I will handle it, the professor and our crowds."

"So, you drew the line at conversation with Marie? That is great, George."

"I reminded people, 'This is an art display, not a talk show. Don't you agree, Howard?"

"I say, listen to Marie! She understands our work, the artistic angle, the scientific angle, your role and the nature of her contribution. She's come a long way. That's all I have to say!"

"She is doing a great job," George nodded.

Howard pointed at the bikini girl poster on the wall behind George, "And she is better looking than this, don't you think George?"

"No comparison! She is the real deal!"

"She attracts more people than DailyFix does," Howard looked around the empty coffee shop.

"Between you and me," George whispered as he looked around the shop. "I overheard the DailyFix owner complaining." He peeked behind the counter to make sure no one was listening. "People who used to get their daily fix at his coffee shop now get it at our Live Art Gallery."

"I suspected that might be the case. But that is not to say people cannot have both their DailyFix coffee and our live art display."

"They want both, but sometimes they cannot have both due to time constraints. I heard them complain about too-short breaks at work."

"Maybe we can help them," Howard said.

"How?" George looked at Howard chewing on a piece

of coffee cake, so George continued, "When the choices need to be made, people choose what they enjoy more."

"I do not believe in sacrifices, George," Howard touched his mouth with his handkerchief.

"What do you suggest, Howard?" George pulled a scrap of paper from his pocket. "You got that fancy pen?"

"In the business world we say if the customer is not coming to you, you go to the customer." Howard produced his Bic pen.

"Can you apply it to our situation?" George asked.

"Maybe we can arrange that DailyFix sells coffee on the street across from the gazebo, or in your yard, if you don't mind."

"Yes!" said George. "They have a cart. I saw it at the Farmer's Market."

"You make the arrangements, George. Consult Frank, so everything is legal," Howard said.

"Of course. Great idea, Howard!"

"No big deal. It is just BNCC."

"What?"

"Businessman's Noble Code of Conduct," Howard translated. "Financially speaking, the more you support other people to succeed, the more you succeed."

George scratched his head. "And here I am, thinking that business people are only taking care of their own bottom line!"

"Oh, George, that is another BNCC."

"Which one?"

"PPV, I think. Personal Preferences Vary."

"True, they do. My personal preference is live art."

"You are not the only one. I noticed some of our viewers are coming back again and again."

"The businessman with the briefcase, college students, three secretaries, the hippies, the artist, the Gypsy girl…." George counted on his fingers.

"Is the Gypsy girl the one I saw you talk to the other day?"

"I had to talk to her. You see, she is a palm reader. I didn't want her distracting our viewers with palmistry. I bought her a cup of coffee, and she read my palm like an open book!"

"That is a correct angle, George. Hundred percent. Keep her out of the crowd." Howard shifted in his chair a little, then moved his head closer to George. "George, I know I wanted to be behind the scenes, but do you think it would be inappropriate for me to take her out to dinner?"

"My Gypsy girl?" George roared. "I don't know…."

"No, George! Marie."

"Marie? Sure, go have dinner with her. She was so apprehensive at the start, and…."

"She seems to be okay now, right?" Howard said.

"She is more at ease, yet I would give her a bit more time, just to make sure."

"I'm in no hurry," Howard touched the corners of his mouth with his handkerchief. "What is a bit more time compared to a lifetime? Nothing."

THIRTY-FIVE

I wasn't ready. Practicing pole dancing for two weeks wasn't enough. But "time and tide wait for no one," as my mom said. I was nervous to the point of quitting, but my body wouldn't quit. My ovulation chart showed a dip. All infertility specialists say you have a 12-hour window. Maybe my last window. Anxiety was debilitating. My body felt stiff. Then I remembered. Very soon after I began seeing Martin, in one of our first and rare discussions about intimacy, he said, "Marie, it may not have been obvious, but I prefer that women approach me. I'm tall and strong and might appear intimidating to women. In the future, don't hesitate to initiate intimacy."

I went to the bedroom and did a bunch of jumping jacks, then put on my $95 silver sparkling bikini I bought for this special occasion. The dent to my savings concerned me, but this was an emergency. You cannot pinch pennies on heart surgery.

I walked into the closet with confidence and grabbed the pole from behind the clothes and marched into the living room. The TV was on. It sounded like the ultimate fighting championship. Martin sat as stoically as ever, his body twitching as if he himself was fighting an imaginary enemy.

At the periphery of his vision, I struck a pose as best I could and stood there for a few seconds. He didn't seem to notice. I made another step forward, and he paid no attention. I was gradually moving dangerously close to the TV screen in front of him, and my subsequent move was noticed.

"What are you doing?" he asked. "You are blocking my view," he made a motion with his hand signaling me to move away. Then, as if he suddenly noticed me, he said, "What's that?"

"I'm working on a routine. I wanted you to see."

By the time I finished the sentence, his eyes had re-focused on the TV screen, and I wasn't sure if he heard me.

"Routine...," I repeated.

"Wait till the commercial break," he said without looking at me.

I stood straight, holding onto the pole resembling a silver monument of some kind.

When the commercials started, he looked at me. "Now, go ahead," he nodded.

Making sure I had enough space, I placed the pole half way between the TV and Martin, and just when I was going to start, I realized I had forgotten my phone and ran to the bedroom.

"Where are you going?" he yelled from the living room. "You are running out of time here."

Running back to the pole, I quickly pulled up my list of songs. I had searched for days for a nice romantic song.

I didn't know what kind of music inspires people to make love. I thought love does. I googled the most romantic songs and selected "When a Man Loves a Woman" and, with the help of my pole dance teacher, created a simple choreography composed of a few figures I practiced.

I selected the song, cranked up the volume, and grabbed onto the pole, waiting. But the song wasn't coming. I glanced at my telephone lying on the floor a meter away from me ready to check on it.

"Marie you have a minute and a half before my show starts," Martin warned me. I froze back in my original position.

Within a few long seconds, a piano tune strangely started softly, so softly I barely could hear, nor recognize. *I'm ovulating, I have no time to waste.* Hesitantly, I started doing a few fireman slides. Finally, to my surprise, the Vienna Boys Choir started singing "Ave Maria."

The music set the mood. I tried to stick to the routine but stretched every move to infinity. The chair spin was difficult to do slowly, so I added a few shoulder rotations, craning my neck, and wiggling my body as much as a swing allowed. Holding onto the pole and doing a pirouette was easy. A knee tuck reflected the emotional flow of the music, so I did it whenever I needed a moment to remember what else I could do. My performance culminated with several cartwheels at the end. Soon I stood again by the pole like a sculpture waiting.

"Wow! You did develop a few muscles," Martin said. "And look at that tan! I cannot believe it," he shook his head and laughed.

I seized that moment to step to him and kneel on the

floor. As I bent and embraced him around the waist, he flinched for a second, and struggled to grab me and pull me up. By the time I unzipped his pants, he stood up, grabbed me and threw me on the couch. "What are you doing?" he hissed through his teeth. "Ambushing me like that!"

I rolled off the couch to the ground, grabbed the pole and ran into the bedroom. If there had been any other room in the apartment, I would have gone there. But there wasn't. I curled on top of the bed in a fetal position and stayed like that for hours it seemed. Didn't matter how hard I tried, it was impossible to avoid the feeling of rejection, like a bird hitting the window glass in full flight, now dead perhaps. The pain of losing another opportunity to have a baby was unbearable. Deep inside I knew this was my last try. I was shaking, either because of being cold, or being shattered. Eventually I backed off the bed to the floor, one knee at a time, as if praying leaning against the bed on my elbows, face down on the ice cold cover.

Embarrassment set in soon. It wasn't fair to do this to Martin. Anger followed. Why did I listen to my mother? What does she know about seducing a man? She had one man her entire life. One man who went to have sex with another woman during their honeymoon. On the other hand, when my mother had difficulties conceiving, he never quit on her. It took them ten years of trying.

I thought, *Okay, this is the end of my baby saga. Life continues. Tomorrow will be a new day. I can't imagine what might happen tomorrow. How do I get up? How do I take a shower and get going without any hope? For sure it is going to be different. Something has changed on a cosmic level. Some balance somewhere in the universe has shifted.* Tears came like a sudden storm. To distract myself, in the darkness I felt around the room for my pajamas, sobbing uncontrollably. They were soft flannel once. Soothing to the skin. I searched on the bed, under the pillows, under the bed, on the chair, in the closet. I couldn't find them. I put on my dress and a hoody, and yoga pants and socks and went under the covers. Still shaking, I pulled the blanket over my head.

THIRTY-SIX

Focused on easily maintaining my posture and neutral attitude towards the entire project, I tried not to look around too much. I was afraid that movements of the crowd, some words spoken in passing, certain angles where my eyes meet another pair of eyes, might re-enliven a doubt.

Yet, as I changed my posture a few times during each session, I could not help but notice under the shadow of a linden tree, the same person seamlessly blending with the greens and browns. I could not tell if it was a man or a woman. At moments when there were not many people around, I looked intensely under the tree, but as the branches moved with the breeze, and as the shadows moved consistently towards me rather than away, I could not solve the mystery.

I tried to avoid direct eye contact with the spectators by looking a bit in the distance. Looking in the distance made it obvious to me that the person who was always under the tree was not there anymore, and I felt somewhat nostalgic as if I had lost a long-known friend. On the same day, an unusual viewer stopped by in front of me and stood looking at me for the entire duration of my session.

Long, somewhat unkempt hair covered the face to a large degree, the skinny figure wore baggy jeans and a plaid shirt hung loose. Not being able to see the face clearly, I was happy to take a couple of glances at the person's hands. I believed hands could tell a lot about a person, but noticed only bony long fingers with long nails and some dirt or paint surrounding the nails. I was disappointed not to be able to learn more about the person, yet I sensed that most likely he was a man.

He stood almost motionless and looked from behind long threads of hair, and when the session was over, he was the last spectator for the day on the property. While George released my hands, the man came closer to the gazebo, and put a piece of paper on the steps leading to the platform on which I was displayed.

As he walked away, I noticed that his hips were slightly rigid and that the knees were bending a bit outward, which convinced me he was a man.

I grabbed the note and took a look. "Artforartsake.com" was the only thing written on it.

As soon as I got into my van, I punched the website into my phone, and found out it was, indeed, a he, Arthur Rubi, an artist. It was apparent he was into nude full-figure portraits.

"So that's it, mystery solved," I said to myself, pumped the gas pedal a few times, ignited the engine, and took off.

I came home around 4 p.m., and since I had an hour available to myself, I got on my laptop and looked at Arthur's website to see his work on a larger screen. He exhibited a lot, in famous galleries in large cities, and there was a sign "sold" under seven portraits, each valued at more than $100,000.

I scrolled to the bottom of the page. He put quotes from the galleries' books of impressions at the bottom: "Rubi sees divine in the form." "Rubi manifests images of grace."

Under the quotes, there was a brief note, "Looking for live models."

THIRTY-SEVEN

When I came back to work next time, the artist Arthur Rubi was already there, sitting on a lawn chair. As I passed by him, he handed me a little piece of scrap paper. Getting to the platform I took a quick peek. "200/hour" it said.

I turned around and nodded at Arthur, crumpled the note and handed it to George, then took my place on the platform.

It was an unusual day at work for me. A TV crew came by. A reporter stood by the gate outside of the yard and talked into a microphone. "It appears that a lightly dressed woman who stays in one place for a time will attract a diverse crowd," I could clearly hear him say. His cameraman filmed at an angle that obviously could include me in the gazebo. This had happened a few times before, but this time I got restless and upset; filming was not part of my agreement. *What if Martin sees it this time?* I was not sure that George could prevent anyone filming outside of the fence, and tried to calm down, hoping that on the screen I would be so far in the background that Martin could not recognize me.

After my session, I found a note on the stairs leading to

the podium. It said "1040 South Street, 4 p.m."

It was already 2 p.m., so I rushed into the van and checked the Google map. South Street was 21 minutes away. I closed my eyes to meditate. The van engine was off, and I kept the window next to me cracked. The sun sifting through the linden tree branches into the van was soothing. In the middle of my meditation, I felt some motion outside of the van right next to me. I waited for a minute sitting with my eyes closed, then looked.

"Hi, George," I said.

"Hi, Marie, sorry to bother you. Are you all right?"

"I'm fine," I said.

I saw you going to your van and was trying to catch up with you to have a chat, but then I saw you had your eyes closed."

"What did you want to talk about?"

"First, I wanted to show you something." He produced a copy of the *Andover Daily News*. "You are on the front page, Marie," he grinned.

"Let me see," I grabbed the papers, *God let me look not like myself!* I prayed inside. I looked at the photo. It was me big as life, no doubt whatsoever it was me!

"Big crowds tomorrow!" said George.

I'd better get to the newspaper before Martin does, I thought. "What else?" I asked.

"Well, it is kind of personal...."

"OK, then join me in my office," I said.

"Didn't know you had an office. Where is it?" he asked.

"Right here," I motioned for him to take the passenger seat.

George laughed as he walked around the van and sat next to me.

"Wow, you can see the insides of this van," he made a move as if he were going to touch a wire on the demolished dashboard.

"Don't touch that wire!" I startled him. George jerked his arm away. "It will blow up the van," I added. He crossed his arms over his chest, his eyes wide open waiting for the explosion.

"Just kidding," I burst into laughter.

"How do you know you are kidding?"

"Well, I don't."

"This sure looks like James Bond's office. You touch something, you don't know what's going to happen."

"Fitto Bar?" I offered the box with a few bars left.

"Sure."

"So what is it you wanted to talk about?" I unwrapped a bar.

"Marie, we would like to tell you we are so happy with your presentation and your professionalism."

"You mean, *all* of you are happy?"

"Yes, all of us," George laughed.

"So nice of all of you. And?" I asked.

"And our secret sponsor would like to take you out to dinner."

"Oh?"

"Yes."

"Why?"

"I think he wants to express his appreciation."

"So nice of him. I cannot refuse, he might feel offended."

"Correct. Besides, he is a nice fellow."

"When?"

"Tomorrow at 7 p.m. He will meet you here."

"Okay."

"That was easier than I thought," George said.

"Is that good or bad?" I asked.

"In this case, it's good. I know him well. He is cool, an old sworn bachelor like me. I'll let you go now. I bet you have a few things to do."

"Yes, it turns out I will have a busy afternoon," I said.

THIRTY-EIGHT

I drove around aimlessly, killing time till 4 p.m. I felt restless and uneasy about my next project, and driving didn't make me feel better. I parked the van by the Oakland Park entrance. I walked as fast as I could straight through the main path, noticing on each side small enclaves with benches and statues of Eros. I found myself walking faster and faster, and then I started running.

Against the colorless canvas of the air, I saw myself the way I was years ago, about two months after I met Martin.

I was sitting next to him on the curb of a street undergoing reconstruction, surrounded by bulldozers and asphalt-mixing machines.

"I cannot go out with you tonight. I know I said I would," he said. *"I cannot waste my time; I am behind my schedule."*

"Okay," I said calmly as if my entire life wasn't crumbling into ruin at that very moment. "What are you going to do?"

"What can I do? This place is stifling me. I want freedom. I want an opportunity to achieve something in life. This is hopeless. You are either blind or too naïve," he said.

"I meant, what are you going to do tonight?"

"Spending all this time with you distracted me from my regimen. I used to be in good shape, now I'm falling apart..."

"So, what are you going to do tonight?"

"Exercise, Marie. I am turning into a slob. I need to exercise."

"Like what?"

"I don't know, Marie. I'll figure out something. Run perhaps. Don't you see? I have to stay strong to survive in this God-forsaken place, spinning my wheels in vain. I need to stay physically and mentally fit, so, should an opportunity come, I can escape."

"I will run with you," I said.

"You mean escape?" He froze.

"I meant run tonight."

"In heels, like that?" he pointed.

"I will go home and change," I decided on the spot.

"I will meet you at the entrance to the park on the west side of town in 30 minutes," he said.

"I would escape too!" I shouted, but he had already disappeared behind a bulldozer.

In high heels and tight skirt, I ran towards the bus stop, nervous I may not be able to make it, either due to the bus being late, or due to pain in my feet, or due to the impossibility of the entire plan. Halfway, I stumbled and stopped. I shifted my purse over my shoulder to free my hands, grabbed the side of my skirt and tore it along the seam up to mid-thigh. This helped me make longer strides. I seriously considered taking off my heels, but didn't want to make my feet dirty, so I decided to endure the pain.

The bus came within the longest ten minutes I ever waited for anything, and after an additional ten-minute ride I got off *the bus and ran towards my house. I kicked off my high heels on the stairs on my way inside. Taking off my sweaty tight blouse and skirt was frustrating. I pulled the drenched bundle from my body with such force I almost tore everything apart. My mother looked at me with her eyes and mouth wide open but said nothing. She knew it was an extreme emergency. I changed into a pair of jeans and a T-shirt, and put on a pair of sneakers, then dashed back to the bus stop, leaving my mother speechless.*

I paced the bus stop and looked as far down the road as I could. Please, please, God, please help me now, I begged. I focused all my energy on the farthest dot in the distance, right at the point at which something is merging with nothing, and I stayed there as if trying to manifest a bus with the sheer power of my gaze.

My attention got caught by an old red Toyota, just like Martin's, driving in the opposite direction. He is looking for me, I thought and waved. The car was going quite fast, but quickly pulled by the curb on the opposite side of the street. He came to pick me up, I thought, my heart beating hard. He knew I couldn't make it and felt my desperation. A flood of feeling of how great, how thoughtful, how loving Martin was, almost choked me to tears. I was so deeply touched by his gesture, I thought I might have a heart attack crossing the street. Not even looking at the driver, I opened the passenger door, hopped on the seat, and threw my arms around his neck.

"Ohh," he said, backing away, looking at me with surprise. I felt something was wrong and looked at him. If I saw a grizzly bear, I would be less surprised than looking into the eyes of a stranger!

I froze for a second. Shockingly and reluctantly, I had to admit it was not Martin.

"Sorry!" I said, got out and slammed the door.

Driven by fear, I ran back to the bus stop, I stood still, paralyzed by the shock. With the edge of my eye I glanced at the red car. The man looked in my direction, shook his head smiling, and drove away.

Finally, the bus appeared. God is gracious to me tonight, I gave a little sigh of relief, yet feeling tension in all my muscles down to my bones.

It took another ten minutes to get back to town, and still I had a long run up the steep street to the park. I hadn't run that long a distance since I was training for 800 meters cross-country on my high school team. I felt my body resisting me and feared I could drop dead at any moment, so I pushed myself to continue. I ran half way to the park fighting back exhaustion at every step.

"Marie," someone yelled from the parking lot. Martin, I thought, *and only because of that hope, without slowing down I looked to the left where the voice came from. A man I had worked with on some projects, whose name I couldn't recall at that moment, waved to me enthusiastically. I waved back without losing a second.*

It already had gotten darker and a single pale star showed in the sky right in front of me. The faint thought He is not going to wait twenty minutes for me *was trying to emerge in my mind, like a mole attempting to pop out of the ground in the whack-a-mole game. I smashed the thought so hard, I think I killed it for good, for it never made another attempt to resurface.*

As soon as I could see the entrance to the park in the distance, I saw a person sitting on the brick support for the sign West Town Park, *about 100 meters ahead of me. I felt my life journey was over,* It's him.

I knew that running fast with sweat seeping into my eyes, and under a faint streetlight fighting the dusk, my capacity to see was fairly low. "Please God, let it be him," I whispered.

Within seconds, I recognized his brown exercise outfit, trimmed with tan trim around the neck, sleeves, and at the hem. I ran towards him, gasping for air. This cannot be just tiredness from running, I thought. I bent down to catch my breath and burst into laughter.

He jumped down from the wall. "Why are you laughing?" he said smiling.

"I just ran for fifty minutes!"

"Let's walk at first till you catch your breath," he said.

He led me in the direction of my home, elegant and graceful with his panther-like movements. He could have taken off and disappeared into the darkness at any moment. But he didn't. Running in front of me he frequently looked back to make sure I followed. About half way from my home, he waited for me to catch up, and lowered himself so I could piggy-back him, and, with me on his back, he alternated between running and walking the rest of the way.

"Come for tea, I got some exotic kind from my godfather."

"Another one?" he smiled.

That kind of smile opens iron doors, I thought, as I ran through Oakland Park back to the van. It was 3:35 p.m., twenty-five minutes before my appointment with Arthur, the artist. I let the air settle down and started driving.

THIRTY-NINE

At 4 p.m., I was in front of 1040 South Street ringing the bell. Arthur opened the door, ceremoniously bowed down and motioned me to come in. His hair covering his face as always, I mused *this could be someone else, I wouldn't know*. He pointed at the shoji screen, and walked in front of me towards it. *This is Arthur's gait no doubt*, I observed.

Behind the shoji screen, I took off my clothes and sniffed my armpits. *Not as bad as it could be*, I thought. The room was warm with a slight scent of candle wax. I peeked from behind the shoji. Arthur had lit a few candles, and the room looked soft and inviting. He spotted me peeking and motioned me to come out. I grabbed my shirt and held it against my body.

He pointed at the pedestal with a wooden cross in the middle of it. I stood right in front of the cross, my back aligned with the vertical beam. Arthur grabbed a bundle of ropes and gently lifted my left arm, extended it along the left side of the horizontal beam, and wrapped the rope around my wrist. He took my right arm, and extended it along the right side of the cross. I dropped my shirt on the floor. He tied the rope around my wrist and knelt in front of me. "Bring your feet together," he said, and tied my ankles to the bottom of the beam.

Arthur stepped back and looked at me the way a microbiologist would look at a new species of algae through a microscope. He walked to the right from the cross to the window and opened the curtain slightly. Still looking at me, he stepped to an easel positioned a few steps to the left from the window and started painting.

Having the experience of standing for hours, and being able to lean against the vertical part of the cross, made it easier for me to maintain the pose. Maybe feeling the physical ease made my mind go to a place of emotional pain.

"How come you are pregnant? Are you sure it's me?" I heard a voice say.

"I don't know. You are the only one I had sex with."

"I'm not ready," he protested. *"There is a way to deal with that,"* he concluded.

A month later I waited for him in front of the hospital, but he never came. "I was having breakfast with a few of my friends," he explained later.

I thought I had gotten over this a long time ago. I was surprised to sense my eyes filling with tears. Rolling down my cheeks, they tickled the front of my neck following the slope between my breasts. Soon my nose started running and I sniffed a few times without changing my posture. Arthur, immersed in his work, showed no signs of noticing anything unusual.

A couple of hours later, my legs started to hurt. As if he knew, Arthur walked towards me, untied my arms and ankles, and handed me a handful of paper-tissues. I sat at the bottom of the cross for a few seconds to blow my nose and regain my composure, then dressed. Arthur walked me to the door and ceremoniously bowed downwards from the waist, his hair bouncing and swaying with his exaggerated motions.

I drove home in an altered state — numb. I ran up the stairs, unlocked the door, and peeked inside. The TV was on. Martin was sitting on the couch, his elbows on his knees, holding widely spread pages of the *Andover Daily News*.

Hesitantly, I got on all fours and crawled towards Martin and snuck between his legs under the paper and continued crawling over his chest until I wrapped my arms around his neck and laid my head on his shoulder.

Behind my back, I heard him quickly fold the newspaper and jam it into his backpack on the floor. "Mousy, I knew it was you." He wrapped his arms around me. "I missed you," he held me tight.

FORTY

As soon as Martin left for work in the morning, I wanted to make a phone call but resisted the impulse and sat to meditate instead. Part of me felt proud for being so diligent with my meditation practice, but another part of me knew better. *It is only 6:30 a.m., they open at 7 a.m.*, I figured.

Time slowed down and stopped, and 20 minutes of meditation was over in a second, it seemed. I lay down silently for a while, then grabbed my phone and found Alpine Business Set-up.

"Good morning, I would like to learn more about your way of doing business," I said.

"What aspect of business set-up are you inquiring about?"

Not being sure how to answer, I said "Financial."

"I will switch you to our loan agents."

I waited, not paying attention to a cacophony of what was supposed to be enjoyable music for callers waiting for the line to be transferred to another department. *Loan agent!* I thought, *that is music to my ears.*

"How can I help you?" I heard a man's voice.

"Do you provide any financial assistance for starting a business?"

"Yes, if you are at the same time hiring our company to equip the business."

"What are the conditions?"

"At least $100,000 down, and the rest would be paid off within 5 years with an interest rate of 7%. You choose the location. Currently, we have set-ups for 15 offices in the broader metro area. You can schedule the tour with the front desk. I can transfer you back, but there could be a few minutes waiting."

"Yes, please," I said.

I waited, the distortion of what in its essence was a perfect piece of music hurting my ears. I thought of my bank account. I have enough for the down payment, but need to make sure I can do the monthly payments until business picks up.

FORTY-ONE

"Marie, you do such a darn good job. I watched you from aside and was amazed that you can stand for two straight hours like that," Howard said, as he led me to his car and held the door open.

"Thank you for the opportunity," I said.

He pulled out of the driveway in front of George's house. "You know we had 216 ladies applying for the job?"

"I didn't know that, but I am not surprised. There are lots of pretty young women who would do it for such a generous rate."

"Yes, but we felt so lucky you came along," he said.

"I bet most of them would have done the job just as well, if not better," I said.

"We didn't think they were the best fit," Howard said.

"How so?"

"Live art means live art, not live modeling, nor live porn, as George would say," said Howard. "May I ask, why did you accept this job?" he added.

"I wanted to help someone financially," I said and looked at the trees along the road. A slight touch of yellow just started to show here and there. "We didn't have rain in a while," I said. "The trees need water."

Howard glanced at the trees, then pulled in front of *Deux Alouettes*, a restaurant serving authentic French cuisine.

Inside, the lights were low. Thick chunky candles glowed everywhere, and Edith Piaf singing "*La Vie en Rose*" was a bit too loud for my ears.

"Marie, I'm a businessman, a straight-shooter, I'm not going to beat around the bush. I will be honest with you," Howard said, as soon as we sat down.

I watched the candle dripping wax onto a silver holder.

"I am a lifelong bachelor," he paused. "Even more importantly, I am a lifelong celibate."

My glance slid from Howard's face onto his chest and down to the white tablecloth upon which Howard's hands, fingers intertwined, were resting. His emerald ring reflected gold arcs from the candle.

"I never thought I would say something like this to anyone, especially to a woman," said Howard. "I have a fulfilling career, I have a nice home. My investment portfolio is getting fatter while we are having our dinner. I have enough resources to do whatever I wish. And I'm happy."

"I never thought I would hear anything like that either," I said.

"Well, there is more," he said. "One day recently, for the first time, I felt that my life was lacking something. I came back home and felt a bit on the empty side. It became clear to me I would like to have someone to share everything I have with."

"That seems reasonable."

"That night when I went to bed, my ivory silk sheets

which I love suddenly felt cold against my skin. Around 2:00 a.m., I woke up from a dream that evoked an intense feeling," Howard paused.

"What was the dream about?" I asked.

"It's heavily raining. I'm walking on the overcrowded sidewalk with my umbrella open, lots of passersby everywhere. As the crowd parted a little, I saw a man sitting on the sidewalk and a woman sitting behind him with her arms wrapped around his chest. The man seems to be in some sort of distress, perhaps injured. People keep stepping in my line of view, and I struggle to discern what is going on. I want to get to them and ask if they need anything, but the crowd keeps stepping in front of me blocking my way. I keep looking in their direction, but the crowd is taking me farther away."

"That was disturbing?"

"I get what I want. I'm lucky. But in the dream, I felt helpless. I am being carried away by the crowd. I keep peeking through, praying to see more. And in a moment, the view clears. It stops raining. Quickly, the sun is shining from behind the clouds. The couple is enveloped in some sort of steam, as if they were sitting on a hot water drainage cover, and I see that the woman is you. You look unreal, almost dissolving into the steam from the hot water. But the expression on your face is so loving, like a mother holding a child."

"That's good, right?"

"It made me feel like I wanted to help."

"You are helping me."

"Then I realized I needed you."

"How can I help you?"

"I would like to have a child with you."

The waiter stepped to the table, "*Bienvenue à Deux Alouettes. Êtes-vous prêt à commander?*"

"*Nous serons prêts dans une minute,*" Howard replied, and looked back at me. "All these years I waited for the right person. I didn't believe that the right person would ever happen. I wouldn't risk a relationship that could hurt my feelings or anybody else's. I never wanted to go through a motion that is solely instinctual. The impulse for procreation is not something I think highly of. I always thought there should be a profound feeling behind two people getting close. But I never felt it. At this point, I'm not sure I ever will. So, Marie," he gestured in a way that included both of us, "I feel this is as close to the purity of physical interaction as I could ever imagine. What do you say?"

"I mean, it's an honor...." I felt like this had happened before. Embracing the lack of fulfillment opens the door to fulfillment. Pieces rearrange themselves as if by magic into a beautiful possibility.

Edith Piaf finished a song I never heard before and started "Milord."

"Marie, I didn't mean to put you in an uncomfortable situation. Let's have a nice dinner and you see how you feel. I am certainly planning to compensate you generously."

"For this?"

"Yes, for this."

"Like companionship?"

"Yes."

"I wouldn't want to be paid for this. I'm not a professional."

"I didn't think you were," Howard said.

The waiter came by and we placed our orders and waited.

The feeling enlivened by Howard's words was not erased nor covered up by casual conversation about weather, chansons, nor Charles Aznavour.

"Marie, do you feel it would be okay if I invite you to my home for tea or dinner, as one might invite a friend?"

"That would be fine."

"Next Friday?"

"Sure."

FORTY-TWO

Howard Blake opened his garage door and drove inside.

"This looks like a public garage," I said, surprised by how spacious it was.

"Almost," Howard laughed.

"Is that a real car, or like a sculpture?" I pointed at a gold sports car.

"A real car! My gold Porsche," Howard said.

"Real gold?" I asked.

"Real gold trim," he answered.

"That must be expensive, I guess."

"$250,000," he said.

I was astonished that such a small car could cost as much as a business. And even more, that instead of investing in a business someone would be inclined to invest in a car that is mostly for show, it seemed.

The car door on my side opened, and Howard stood there extending his bent elbow for me to take, "The entrance is straight ahead," he laid his palm on the top of my arm.

"To the right is the game room. Pool, video machines, card tables, darts, and ping pong," Howard pointed as soon as we entered the house. "There's miniature golf in the basement."

I looked around the room the size of a basketball court.

"Do you play games?" he asked.

"Not that I am aware of."

"What do you do for fun?" he asked.

"I try to find fun in everything I do."

"Successfully, I would assume."

"I would not assume such a thing."

"You exercise?" He asked.

"I run."

"Often?"

"As needed, I would say."

"You have a nice figure," he said without scanning my body. "You must be doing something right."

"Yoga and meditation," I said.

He led me to a large mahogany-paneled dining room with a long wide dining table set with crystal glasses, china cups and plates.

"Ready for supper?" he asked and pulled out my chair. "Please help yourself with the hors'd'ouvres," he motioned towards glass bowls filled with sliced carrots, celery sticks, radishes, and olives, then walked away along the table.

"Are you leaving?" I asked.

"No!" he laughed. "Just wanted you to enjoy the roses. They are for you!" From the opposite end of the table he picked up two vases filled with red roses and placed them to my right, then sat across from me.

"Thank you," I said.

"Marie," he looked into my eyes, "Do you feel comfortable talking to me openly, without reservation?"

"Yes, I do," I nodded.

"I would like to know what is happening inside of you while you stand in the gazebo."

"Mostly nothing," I said.

"No thought, no feeling?" he asked.

"For the most part," I said.

"Is it because you embrace your role as a piece of art? Like a painting or a sculpture?"

"Maybe."

"Were there moments when a feeling did come?"

"I remember a few weeks ago, a sparrow landed on my head. It moved around and flapped its wings. A mother and a child stood in front of me. The child said, 'Look, Mommy, look, a birdie!' He kept pointing with his little index finger. Through his eyes, I saw a world of wonders opening up in my heart. Infinite space filled with light flowing like water and air blended in a reflection of soft music that I heard in his voice chirping, 'She can fly, Mommy! She's got wings.' Then I knew air and water would support me. Why are you asking?"

"All this time," he said, "about a year now, I kept watching you standing in the gazebo. At first, I just wondered why are all these people so much in need to look at the bikini woman. And while I was preoccupied with the phenomenon, it happened that I talked to a fellow who enlivened within me deeper layers of reality of seeing. I noticed how seeing more enlivens the feelings, and with the feelings lively within, you see more without."

He paused. I dipped a slice of carrot in garlic dip and crunched it.

"There was a moment when the sun was right in your

eyes, and the wind blew your hair over your face, and the droplets of sweat or tears were rolling down, and you just stood there. Breathing. And I wondered, what were you feeling?"

I looked for something smart to say but found myself disassociated from my brain. "I don't know what I felt at that particular moment," I stumbled, "but normally in such a situation, I would extend my lower jaw and direct my breath up, to blow my hair away from my face." I demonstrated.

"Ha ha ha," Howard laughed, "Now when I think of it, you might have done such a thing."

"I just came up with it, and it seems to be true."

"What I saw, Marie, was as if your upper lip twitched a little, and there was a moment of suspense, and it was difficult to say whether you were going to cry or smile." He looked at me and waited. I didn't know what to say. I was forced to embrace my brainlessness, so I silently looked back. "That moment stayed with me," he whispered.

The kitchen door opened, and the cook rolled in a serving cart loaded with hot steaming food.

"Hey, Justin," Howard waved casually to the cook. "Thank you for working on your day off."

"No, Mr. Blake, thank you for paying me twice my rate."

Howard rearranged a few items on the table to create space for Justin to place the dishes. "Justin, you outdid yourself again, that's why I love you."

"Money inspires me like nothing else, Mr. Blake, I assure you," Justin said, as he rolled the empty serving cart back to the kitchen.

"Please help yourself, Marie. A good sense of humor is not his greatest gift, trust me. Gravy?"

"Sure."

Howard poured gravy over my mashed potatoes.

I took a mouthful. "Simple food, but such a unique flavor."

"The secret is in the pomegranate sauce." Howard touched the corners of his mouth with a linen napkin. "Where were we?" He looked at me.

"The moment stayed with you," I reminded him.

"Like a ... I almost said like a shadow, but it was more real."

"Meaning?"

"It wasn't haunting, coming and going, but had more like a constant presence."

"A presence?"

"In the sense that it was always there. So much so that I started feeling as if it was me, not you."

"Was it like a memory?"

"If it was, it would be like a memory of something that never happened, that I never knew."

"Something you never knew about yourself?"

"Yes."

"What was it?" I stared at Howard.

"A feeling of feeling someone's feelings based on the wind blowing a strand of hair...." Howard looked at the half-burned candle. "I will forever be indebted to you."

"I would like to take credit, but I did nothing."

"I learned recently that it is not about doing, but being," he said.

"Still, being is not my doing, but thank you," I said.

"It is all your doing, Marie." He paused. "There were times that I had spoken about women and love with arrogance. It never struck me that it was about me."

"What was it about you?"

"Just the lack of experience. Once I had the experience, I knew. And what I knew was that tender feeling about someone. So tender in fact, that it was me."

I tried to wipe off a tear before Howard saw it, but it was too late. He walked around the table and knelt on the floor beside me. Before I could stop him, he took my face in his hands, and wiped off my tear, then went back to his seat.

"There is so much there, Marie," he touched his chest.

"Can you name it?"

"Love!" he said, "that love of money and cars cannot hold a candle to."

"Why?"

"Because objects cannot mirror the soul."

"Why?"

"Too much solidity. Only human beings have the same fluid matrix beneath the seeming solidity of the body," he said.

"Love is a state of being," I said. I had no idea I could say such a thing. "It is not about how much we are being loved and adored. It is how much of love we can feel towards others, and that would be the amount of love we can recognize in others for us, and therefore be able to appreciate."

Howard shook his head and smiled, "I understand now why they say love is sublime."

"It is sublime! Or it is not."

"The candle's burned almost down," Howard said, and put out the flame with his bare fingers, the way my mother does, just without licking his fingers first. "Come, I'll take you home. It's getting late."

FORTY-THREE

I wasn't sure what Howard's idea of closeness or friendship was. He was willing to look deep into things, and I liked that. He appreciated me in a way I do not think anyone else could, not that I was looking for appreciation.

In a moment of confusion or weakness, when I wasn't clear that what I was doing was right, I might have needed exterior confirmation. I tried a few times to get it from Namaste. But Namaste didn't say much. Not more than 'Life is such…' or 'All is unbounded awareness' or 'Nothing is good or bad.' He came up with such final statements, against which any further discussion was futile. He gave a general answer to a specific concern, which was no answer. Still, in a weird way, no answer worked for me. No answer was an answer. Doubt is always in a detail. Specific answers work on the level of doubt, while general answers expand the understanding and therefore distract from the doubt, bringing relief.

Talking with Howard is like a scene from a play.

"Howard, I love your library," I looked at shelves packed with books. "Books used to be my best friends," I nestled in the cushions of a white wingback chair.

"How so?" Howard put the tray with tea-kettle, cups and saucers on a small table, then sat in the armchair opposite from me.

"How so?" I echoed, leaned my head back, and closed my eyes for a few seconds. "I looked for something to relate to on a deeper level."

"Tell me more," Howard said.

"There was a hole right here," I touched my chest, "and the emptiness would stir up from time to time."

"This emptiness, did it come from something outside of you?"

"There is no such thing as outside. Everything is inside," I said and paused. *Namaste would be proud of me*, I thought.

"Aha!" Howard sipped his tea. "Emptiness, how does it feel?"

"It feels like a kind of isolation that rarely gets reduced by being around people."

"But it can be reduced by reading?"

"Reading gives more opportunities to feel the deep connection that brings a sense of fulfillment." I looked at the bookshelf to my right and pulled out a book. "*Anna Karenina*! When I was eighteen, I dreamed about Anna looking into her own love and seeing her love as a part of her, independent of the object of her love. I saved her from her fate many times in my dreams. Once she even looked at me with teary eyes and said, *"Dieu merci, ma chère."*

"Anna was beautiful and passionate."

"Yet her emotional satisfaction was on hold," I said. "She was a beautiful, attractive, energetic woman who was shriveling up inside while waiting for a man in her life to fill the void. Her husband was preoccupied with his career and, except for social status and stability, had nothing to give her. Vronsky, at his age, naturally would not be able to bring substance into her life. And we can have a discussion whether providing material resources means love, and whether desiring is the same as loving."

"It can be," Howard said, "if you take care of someone's financial well-being out of love for them, and not out of the need to make them yet another possession to display to the world, like my Porsche. More tea?" he offered.

"Yes, please."

"And the love of flesh can arise from the love of person," he continued. "If it does, it invariably lasts and doesn't fade over time."

"True. Deep in her heart Anna knew that the financial stability her husband provided was spurred by his sense of responsibility, self-worth, and pride that he was a responsible citizen."

"He did what he was supposed to do," Howard said.

"True, in a financial sense. He could have given her a bit more attention, though. And that is where the doubt that he loved her crept in, and the feeling he loved only himself became a possibility," I said. "He needed her the way he needed his house, his position, his social status. Who she was, or what she dreamt of, he gave no importance to. She was an important part of his picture of himself and his role in society, not more than that."

"Marriage was considered a business arrangement at that time, and might still be to a large degree." Howard sipped his tea.

"I see no problem with that if it works for both parties. It doesn't need to exclude mutual love and respect, though," I said.

"Could Vronsky's passion for Anna be considered love?" Howard asked.

"Yes, if it never changed."

"It didn't change for him," Howard said.

"Anna thought his love was out of vanity."

"It is difficult for men, trying to prove their worth in a society that judges individuals based on false criteria of manhood," said Howard.

"Love is not for what other people do or don't do, it is more about who they are."

"True, some people love more, some love less," Howard agreed.

"And love is not based on reciprocity either: if you love me, I love you; and if you don't, I don't."

"How do you love someone who doesn't love you back?" Howard asked.

"Can we know for sure we are not loved back?"

"We know when we are not treated lovingly, don't we?"

"You know they love you to their individual maximum, and mistreatment is coming from unhappiness within them, which arises from their inability to love more."

"We shouldn't be in a relationship with those who don't treat us kindly," Howard said.

"Yet we can still love them, regardless," I said.

"If Anna and Vronsky couldn't have a perfect love, who could?" Howard said.

"Maybe spending a decade in a loveless relationship made her doubt the possibility of love," I said. "Even while experiencing love, Anna questioned it, and saw herself separate from it."

"Can love even have a chance, considering how dysfunctional people are?" Howard touched a corner of his mouth with his napkin.

"Yes, if you look at love as something you find within yourself," I said.

"We want to find love outside of ourselves because that makes us feel worthy as humans," Howard said. "We want to say 'I love you' to someone, and we want to give credit to someone else for what we feel, like they make us love them by being who they are."

"If that were true, then the same person who made us love them could make us not love them."

"You think love should last forever or otherwise it is not love?" Howard asked.

"I am saying that love has to come from within, and it has to be unconditional, and only then it is not going to turn into sorrow," I said.

"Vronsky loved Anna and was devoted to her, yet she doubted that, and that is why their love didn't bring her fulfillment. I find that sad," Howard said.

"Me too," I agreed. "She had limitations."

"Limitations cause suffering?" Howard asked.

"We are created to live to our full capacity, so limitations are a pinch. Yet the power of love is so great that even a little of it brings joy," I said.

"How so, when we just said if it is within limitations it causes suffering?"

"Love has life and power of its own greater than limitations. It replenishes itself as the heart overflows with it."

"You said it in a poetic way, Marie," Howard smiled.

"I cannot take credit; I heard it from a wise teacher."

"Still, you are a wise student to see the wisdom of it."

"Thank you, Howard," I smiled. "I appreciate your appreciation."

"You are welcome," he said. "Love knows no reason." He finished his tea.

"And if love does know a reason, is it still love?" I asked.

"Some kind I would guess, maybe a short-lived kind, maybe a long-lived kind, just a different kind," Howard looked at our empty tea cups, "There is still plenty of hot tea in the kettle. Want some more?"

"Yes, please," I held out my cup. "When I get in tune with my heart, I feel that love for love's sake is a true love, the only love that has a real chance."

"Why do you think that?" Howard poured the hot tea.

"It transcends reason. It transcends the limitations of our context. Being in love with the way you love someone is being in love with love, which is ultimate loving."

"Is that how you love?" he asked.

"That is how I aspire to love."

FORTY-FOUR

I had a slight feeling as if something out of the ordinary was happening during my gazebo hours. For a second, I saw Howard walk along the street. There was nothing in his behavior that suggested something was wrong. He looked calm and composed and focused. Except that he was pacing.

George walked towards the gazebo, and I looked at him trying to see an explanation on his face, but he shrugged and smiled and gave me thumbs up. I looked up and down the street as far as I could, and I looked all over the yard, but Howard was not to be seen. *Maybe it was not Howard after all*, I thought.

While George untied the leather cuff bracelets on my wrists, one at a time, I asked, "Did Howard stop by?"

"Have not seen Howard today," George said, checking the rope in the O-ring on the first bracelet before hanging it through the silver ring on a post.

"Here, you are a free woman again." He hung the second bracelet and its rope through the silver ring on the opposite post.

I went to the van. I don't know if I had gotten some

muscle power from eating Fitto Bars, or if I had developed a better method of slamming the door, but I was much better in getting the door shut on the first try. I looked at the clock. It was 2:24 p.m.

I closed my eyes and meditated.

About twenty minutes later, I opened my eyes. Thoughtless, I focused my gaze on a stain on the windshield, located on the top left corner of a crack, where a big bug hit the glass and left a blotch. With the sunlight radiating through it, the blotch looked like a goldfish.

"I am not ready for marriage," I remembered Martin saying. *"My income is not enough, and you're still in school. You had all this time to finish your degree. How come you couldn't finish it?" he said.*

"I have only comprehensive exams to complete. Besides, I started shelving books at the University library," I said.

"I know. I know. Something totally useless to me. Menial work for minimal pay," he said. "Maybe fashion modeling, but you do not have the height. There is something that pays more and no experience needed," he paused. "Young girls put themselves through college by posing nude for magazines or the Internet. You do have the body for that. It would take some research to get started, but in the meantime, I do not want us to be on welfare," he said.

Maybe he wouldn't mind, I thought, looking through the goldfish down the street framed with linden trees.

As I pumped the pedal three times, I saw George in the rearview mirror running toward the van with a big package under his arm. I rolled my window down. "Marie, this is for you," he said.

"Who is it from?"

"I don't know. It doesn't say."

I looked at the flat, six-by-four-foot package wrapped in coarse brown paper, tied with heavy string and a gold ribbon. "Are you sure it's for me?"

"The card has your name on it, Marie."

"Let's put it in the back," I said.

"See you tomorrow," he said, and slammed the rear door.

I pumped the gas, turned on the ignition, and drove off.

I parked the van by Namaste's house, turned around, and looked at the package in the back of the van, the gold ribbon tied into a big bow around the middle, and the card with my name on it. I grabbed the envelope and opened it.

It was a blank card with no picture. Inside, it said, "To Marie, my divine divinity."

"My divine divinity?" I shook my head, got outside the van, and opened the back door.

I tried to find where the wrapping paper was taped so I could unwrap the package without tearing the paper, which itself felt stiff and sturdy. The packaging tape was strong and would not peel off easily. Forcefully, I tore the paper apart.

"No!" I whispered. "Me?"

There was my naked slim body crucified, twisted in discomfort. The blood dripping from my feet and hands. A glistening stream of tears running down my cheeks. My nose red and runny. My mouth half open like a fish gasping for air.

I looked deeper. Somewhere under the surface expression of pain, there was a feeling of ease of embracing destiny, the ease of letting go. I felt my eyes welling up with tears of joy. Looking at the painting, I felt release from the boundaries of what I thought was considered normal or customary. As if conventional concepts of pleasure and pain lost validity.

The words, "my divine divinity," lit up my awareness. Although it seemed unusual that Arthur would say such a thing, I was touched by his expression and so it felt natural. I felt he genuinely saw me as a divine being, yet I had done nothing to make him think that way. I knew it was more his perception of me than me. Artists have a unique vision of the world. Still the words caused a little shift. I felt I could just be Marie and that being Marie would be not only enough, but a lot.

I cannot have Martin see this, I thought, and started feeling nervous, as if someone was watching me.

I looked around, hoping I was not getting paranoid. Bent over the orchids blooming on his east window, holding a spray bottle in his hand, Namaste was watching me. I didn't know if from his position he could see me naked in the painting. With the back of my hand I quickly wiped off my tears, and conjured a smile as I rushed to cover the nude picture with torn pieces of wrapping paper.

It was obvious that it would be impossible to connect the pieces of the wrapping paper into one piece large enough to cover at least certain delicate parts of my body without taping the pieces onto the painting. I flipped the painting upside down, so that the back of it was facing up. *This should work for the time being*, I thought, and peeked through the car window. Namaste was spraying his orchids. When he looked at me, I motioned him to come to the car, pointing at the package. He nodded and came out quickly, as if he had walked straight through the wall.

"Can you store this for me for a while?" I asked.

"Sure," he said, and grabbed the picture. "No big deal!

Man is an exact image of God. Our body is our temple, it is divine," he mumbled, carrying the painting towards his house.

As I walked towards the curb to wait for Martin, I googled Arthur's website, and punched his number into the phone. He didn't answer. I left a message.

"Hi Arthur. So nice of you to deliver the painting of me to the Live Art Gallery, with such a heartfelt note. I am deeply touched by your painting and by your words. Unfortunately, I am not in a position to keep the painting at this time due to my living circumstances. I believe there must be a better place for your art, where people would be able to enjoy it. Let me know where you would like me to drop it off, and I would be happy to do so."

Soon, the red CRV emerged from behind the curve, and I felt content.

"Mousy Mouse, don't slam the door," Martin greeted me.

FORTY-FIVE

I felt drops of sweat trickling down my neck and back. I could manage the tickling, as long as people were not close enough to notice I was sweating.

After an additional hour in the sun, the linden tree shadow migrated in my direction and slowly started climbing up my leg. By that time, the hair around my face and neck felt drenched as if I just took a shower. The drops of sweat were rolling down my chest between my breasts and down my belly, getting absorbed by the fabric of my bikini, leaving darker marks.

A group of about fifteen young people gathered around the gazebo, talking to each other and taking pictures with their cellphones. *An art class*, I guessed.

Within an hour the tree shadow had reached my thighs, and I could feel my body slowly cooling down a few degrees.

By the time George came to untie the ropes, I felt I could continue standing there till dark.

"Marie, I hope you don't mind, we booked you for a photo shoot with one of the visitors. She teaches photography at MST Institute."

"I saw people taking pictures. I assume she could do the same."

"She wants to document our event but also wants a private photo shoot with you in her studio."

"I don't know about the private photo shoot, never done it," I said.

"She said she pays $600 per session, and wants to reserve the right to use the pictures any time she wishes."

I needed a lot more money to bankroll Martin's start-up. "George, please tell her I'll do the photo shoot for $1,000. What do you think?"

"I will text her and see if she accepts." George hung each leather bracelet and its rope through a silver ring on each post, typed into his cellphone, then walked with me towards the van.

"See you tomorrow," George said and closed my van door. As he started turning around to leave, he noticed the door bounced back open.

I sat in the driver's seat, looking at Gorge, rolling my eyes, shaking my head, and drumming my fingers against the steering wheel.

George banged the door harder, and watched it open yet again.

"George, have no mercy!" I encouraged.

Before George made an attempt to repeat the process, his telephone rang. He checked the phone.

"Photo shoot tomorrow at 6 p.m., $1,000 okay," George read from his text. "I will forward you her address. Maybe you should bring a friend, it is not a safe area," he added.

"I will see what I can do. Thanks, George," I grabbed the door and slammed it so hard I saw the neighborhood cat dive into a juniper bush.

FORTY-SIX

I walked in front of Namaste's house looking for the van while rummaging through my purse for my cellphone. I fished it out and dialed.

"Namaste! Can't find your van."

"In the shop around the corner. Ignition stopped working, They just called, it's fixed," he said on the phone.

"I have to go to a bad part of town, can you go with me?"

"My routine would not accommodate such an excursion, Besides, there is no good and there is no bad, there is no high and there is no low."

"There isn't?"

"There isn't."

I looked around one corner and couldn't see the shop. *This is taking too long,* I thought.

"On the opposite side," he said.

"Thank you, Namaste," I said surprised, looking in the direction of Namaste's house now blocked from my vision by a large abandoned storage building. I touched my forehead with the back of my palm. *I am perspiring, this cannot be good,* I thought.

"There is neither good, nor bad," I heard Namaste say.

"And there is neither high nor low…" I said and pushed the end button on my phone.

I rushed around the corner on the opposite side and could see the van parked in front of a shop. I opened the door, saw the key in the ignition, and looked around. The mechanic lifted his head from under the hood of a pickup truck, and showed me thumbs up. I started the engine and pushed the gas pedal. The engine roared and I took off, glancing at the directions on my phone.

Out of breath I ran into a downtown brick building with a big ADIOS graffiti on it. "Sorry I am a bit late," I said to the woman dressed in a black body suit standing in the lobby.

"Over there, that room across the lobby. You can change. I left your costume on the chair," the woman said and disappeared.

I stepped into the room and noticed a black leather bikini draped over the chair and high-heel over-the-knee boots scrunched under the chair.

"What?" I whispered. "Bikini again?"

I put on the black leather bikini and put on the high-heel, black leather boots and, barely able to walk, stood in the middle of the room looking in a mirror.

"Ready for the makeup?" a voice startled me. A man carrying a plastic box entered the room. "Here," he pulled the chair in front of the mirror, and placed the box on a counter top.

The makeup artist worked fast, moving about in a very experienced manner. He put an enormous bunch of colorful feathers in my hair and did an extreme eye makeup making my eyes slanted and elongated like they did in Egypt. *Cleopatra would be jealous*, I thought, looking in the mirror.

"Ready for the shooting?" a voice called behind me.

Without saying anything, I followed the woman into a fully lit studio decorated with large bright yellow lacy parasols.

Whatever the demand was, I adjusted easily and morphed flawlessly with the bright environment on the set. As time passed, my lips got parched from the heat and thirst, but I felt neither resistance nor fatigue.

"Set change break. We will continue in thirty minutes," someone said.

I picked up my purse and looked at my phone to check messages. Arthur left a message. Martin called two times without leaving a message, which meant he needed me. The moment I thought of calling Martin back, I felt the phone vibrating in my hand.

"Hello Martin."

"I was going to..."

"What are you going to? ... The reception is bad here."

"I am taking a CE class... and ..."

"Hold, just a second, I am walking outside to see if the reception is better."

"...It is about bonding..." he said.

"About bonding! Really?" My face lit up with a smile. "What did they say about bonding, sweetie?" I asked, surprised and touched that Martin had taken the initiative. I walked out onto the sidewalk with only a few distant streetlights on.

"Some new technique..." he said.

"Technique?" I gasped and stepped on the edge of the

curb staring into the darkness.

"… Fast-acting etchant and primer in one," he said.

The nearest streetlight reflected against the shiny surface of my leather bikini. *Probably fake*, I thought. "Oh, nice. You like it?"

"Of course I do, but where I am right now I have no chance of utilizing the top-notch technology, as you know," Martin said.

"I know."

I switched the cellphone screen to my bank account. *Without a steady income, I cannot risk taking on monthly payments*, I admitted to myself with a flinch.

"I have to go back, they are starting the hands-on session," Martin said.

"Enjoy, we will talk later at home. Love you." I disconnected.

If I pay $100,000 down, I will still have $25,000 left, which would be enough for four monthly payments. Still, it would be risky. The gazebo display might end at some point, for any number of reasons, forcing me to find other work, I thought, and switched to Arthur's message: "Dear Marie, I wish I could take credit for everything, especially for the note you liked. I did not send the painting to you. A rich dude commissioned the portrait and compensated me amply…."

A silver Mercedes SUV pulled right in front of me by the curb.

"Need a ride?"

"No, I am kind of working," I said, pointing at the building behind me.

"I thought so," the man smiled.

"… Selling that portrait would be easy," Arthur's message continued. "Look at my website for clues how much my work goes for, add twenty-five thousand on account of high demand. If you make the decision to sell, I could get as much as $125,000 for that portrait for you, if you want. I know a buyer."

"$1,000 for a night?" the man in the silver Mercedes said.

"What?" I was surprised he was still there.

"$1,500?" he said.

I bent down and looked questioningly at the driver through the open passenger window.

"Okay, $5,000 with a video recording," the man smiled.

"$10,000," I heard myself say. Good, I thought, *no one would go for that.*

"Ten thousand, and I reserve the distribution rights." The man opened the door and motioned me to come inside, "Step into my office," he said.

" That is my line," I smiled.

As I held the car door open with one hand, suddenly from out of a seemingly clear sky, rain came down with richness. I looked up feeling the raindrops cooling my face rolling down like tears. The cell phone in my hand vibrated continuously, it seemed. I scanned the message, "Marie, I know you want to help. We will be okay, we have each other."

END